# A SCREAM IN THE NIGHT

Beyond the city, air was pleasantly cool and much less muggy. Once Zach was on the lonely stretch of road to the Wilkerson estate, the night, and the swampland, closed in around him. The swamp pulsed and throbbed with the croaking of frogs and the chirping of crickets, to say nothing of the many grunts, screeches, cries and snarls that rose in feral chorus.

Zach stuck to the middle of the road. Alligators sometimes came out on land and he would rather not blunder into one in the dark.

Distant bright rectangles gave Zach some idea of how far he had to go. He kept expecting a carriage to come along but none did. When he was within five hundred yards of the high walls, he slowed. He must not be spotted.

Zach was debating whether to slip through the swamp and come up on the estate from the north or the south when a new sound keened as stridently as the shriek of a panther, a sound that momentarily hushed the frogs and crickets and other creatures of the night and formed a ball of gnawing anxiety in the pit of Zach's stomach. There was no mistaking it for anything other than what it was; the scream of a woman, or a young girl, in dire terror.

The *Wilderness* series:

# #44
# WILDERNESS
## SHADOW REALMS

# David Thompson

LEISURE BOOKS  NEW YORK CITY

*For Judy, Joshua, and Shane.*

A LEISURE BOOK®

December 2004

Published by

Dorchester Publishing Co., Inc.
200 Madison Avenue
New York, NY 10016

ISBN 0-8439-5256-3

The name "Leisure Books" and the stylized "L" with design are trademarks of Dorchester Publishing Co., Inc.

Printed in the United States of America.

Visit us on the web at www.dorchesterpub.com.

# #44
# WILDERNESS

## SHADOW REALMS

# Chapter One

Alain de Fortier strolled jauntily out of Le Grande and ran a manicured finger along his rapier-thin mustache. He adjusted his hat at a rakish angle and his cloak about his wide shoulders, then turned to bend his steps for home.

Just then a handsome carriage rattled around the corner and came to a stop before the ornate double doors with their bronze trim and tinted glass. Henri, the doorman, was quick to open the carriage door and hold out his arm to assist the occupants in climbing down.

Fragrant perfume wreathed Alain de Fortier in a tantalizing cloud, perfume he knew all too well, and he removed his hat as a shapely ankle was lowered and a beauteous wonder settled to earth with the grace and allure of the most dazzling butterfly. Alain bowed and smiled. "*Bonsoir*, Gemma. This is indeed both a great surprise and a marvelous honor."

1

The young lovely so addressed did not return his smile. Fluttering her fan in the humid evening air, she cast a withering glance, her green eyes dancing with fire. "I should well imagine it is a surprise since you believed me to be at my father's estate. As for the honor, I should think that someone who has neglected to call on me for over a month can hardly be interested."

Alain unfolded and replaced his hat with a flourish. "*Non*, mademoiselle. I assure you that you could not be more mistaken. Only the most pressing business could keep me from your doorstep."

Gemma sashayed nearer, her fan fluttering faster, her eyes burning brighter. "Business, is it? What sort of *business* did you have with that silly Elizabeth Ordinay two weeks ago? What *business* kept you overnight at the Ortega hacienda when Senor Ortega was away? And was it *business* you discussed with that harlot from the tavern until the small hours of the morning three nights ago?"

"I am shocked," Alain declared, and truly was. "Have you been spying on me?"

"Don't flatter yourself, peacock," Gemma said haughtily. "Of what interest would your escapades be to me? A girl hears things, is all."

Alain placed a hand to his chest. "You pierce my heart, my dear. From the day we met you have been uppermost in my thoughts."

"Spare me that glib tongue of yours. You had your chance, and in the parlance of the street, you blew it. I would no more deign to go out with you again than I would with a darkie."

"You misjudge me, mademoiselle," Alain said, but Gemma moved past him and motioned for Henri to open the copper-gilt doors for her. "Might I call on you tomorrow night to prove I am in earnest?"

"Should you ever set foot on our estate again," Gemma said without looking at him, "I will have the dogs sicced on you, and if you live, I will have you thrown into the swamp for the alligators to feed on. Do I make myself clear?"

"*Oui*," Alain said.

"And do you believe me, Monsieur de Fortier?"

"If I have learned anything from our association, mademoiselle," Alain said, "it is that you are a woman of your word." He turned to go and almost collided with the other occupant of the carriage, who had stepped down and stood demurely waiting to follow her sister inside. "Rachelle! My apologies. I did not realize you were there."

"That is quite all right, monsieur," Rachelle said. "I am quite accustomed to not being noticed." Her hair was black, not golden like Gemma's, her face plainer, her dress did not cost half as much.

"Anyone who would not notice you is a fool," Alain said with more vehemence than was prudent, and to cover himself, he quickly asked, "How have you been keeping yourself?"

"I am fine, thank you," Rachelle said softly. "I keep busy, what with Gemma dragging me off to every function under the sun." She glanced skyward. "And the moon too, at times."

Alain laughed and almost reached for her hand. "You always bring a smile to my lips. Have you finished that novel you were so interested in when last I saw you?"

"*Barnaby Rudge*? Yes. The writer, Mr. Dickens, shows great promise." Rachelle's eyes lit with a fire completely different from her sister's. "Last night I read the most wonderful story, by an American, a gentleman called Poe. He is gifted with a most singular grasp of the macabre."

"And you, if I may be so bold, are gifted with a most singular eloquence," Alain complimented her.

Rachelle blushed and bowed her chin. "Oh, monsieur. It is not nice to tease a lady like that."

"Who is teasing?" Alain responded, and would have said much more but just then Gemma intruded.

"Come along, Rachelle. The next performance is in fifteen minutes and I do not intend to miss it."

Giving a slight curtsy, Rachelle rustled past Alain. "I am sorry, monsieur. For what it is worth, I have enjoyed these brief moments very much."

Alain could only stand and stare as Gemma hustled Rachelle off. He glanced at Henri, whose face might as well have been sculpted from stone, and muttered, "*Les femmes*, eh?" Swirling his cloak about him, he marched off, forgoing his usual saucy swagger, bound for the waterfront district. He was so deep in thought that he did not notice the mistake he had made until a pair of badly scuffed boots barred his path.

"What have we here? A fancy gentleman in all his finery."

Looking up, Alain beheld three men, river rats by the look of them, as scruffy and dirty as their namesakes. Long knives hung from each wide belt, and one rat was fingering a hilt. "What's this then, gentlemen?" Alain asked, masking his dismay at finding that somewhere or other he had taken a wrong turn and was on a cobblestoned side street he would ordinarily avoid.

"I hear tell gentlemen like yourself have good manners," said a barrel-chested knave with a bushy beard and dark, piglet eyes. "So how about you prove it and give us some drinking money?"

"You must be jesting," Alain said. Under his cloak, his hand found the hilt of his sword.

"Do you see me laughing, mister?" the man said, and held out a callused hand. "Hand over your poke and you can be on your way."

"Subtle, aren't we?" Alain said, and took a step back. A low cough behind him was the first inkling he had that four more footpads were to his rear. "Seven against one? That's hardly fair."

"Your poke," the big one persisted. "Unless you would rather we take it by force." His blade glinted wickedly in the twilight. It was the signal for the others to draw theirs.

"I don't suppose if I offered to spare your lives that you would go on your way and pester someone else?" Alain politely asked.

The big one snorted. "I'll remember that one when we're drinking a toast over your grave. Now be a good gent and toss your money here before we lose our tempers."

"Wait!" a tall scalawag exclaimed. "We have a witness!" And he pointed.

Where the newcomer came from, Alain could not say. One moment he was not there; the next he was, standing partly in shadow. He appeared to be wearing fringed buckskins, which was unusual but not uncommon, and beaded moccasins, which was unusual and uncommon.

"Make yourself scarce, stranger," the big footpad commanded. "This is none of your affair."

When there was no reply, the tall one said, "You heard him. Be on your way or rue your stupidity."

The man stepped out of the shadows. He was younger than Alain, perhaps in his early twenties. A mane of raven black hair hung past his shoulders. His features were nearly as dark. Alain could not decide whether it was a trick of the light or whether the man might be part Creole or even Indian. A beaded sheath was attached to his belt, and judging by its size, the knife the sheath held had to be a bowie.

"Cat got your tongue, boy?" the big robber gruffly demanded. "Or are your ears so plugged with wax you can't hear?"

The youth finally spoke. "I hear fine."

"Then why aren't you doing as you've been told?" The big one's piglet eyes narrowed, then blazed with spite. "Wait a minute. You're a damned breed."

"So?" the young man said.

"So breeds don't have the sense God gave a jackrabbit. I've yet to meet one who didn't have horse shit coming out his ears."

At that the others cackled, and the tall one and one other moved toward the half-breed. "What do we have to do, boy?" the tall one taunted. "Put you over our knee and spank you?"

"You will all die," the breed said.

That stopped them. The tall one looked to the barrel-chested one and motioned as if to say, "Do we do it?"

"You will all die," the young breed repeated, "and I will drink a toast to ridding the world of five jackasses."

Alain realized the stripling was mocking them, that he was throwing their own words back in their faces, and he grinned at the sheer boldness of it.

The tall cutthroat hissed like a viper and sprang. He was fast, this one, but as fast as he was, the young half-breed was faster. The bowie leaped from its beaded sheath and sliced the air in a silvery blur. The tall one staggered, a fine red mist spurting from the slit that stretched from ear to ear. He squeaked like a mouse and clasped a hand to his neck, but he could not stem the geyser. He tried to run, but after several faltering steps, his knees gave way and he collapsed, mewing in his death throes.

The others were transfixed in disbelief and horror. They looked at the young breed, at the blood dripping from his blade. Their horror changed to hate, and uttering an oath, another leaped to finish the job the tall one had started. Steel rang on steel.

Alain was being temporarily ignored. He remedied that by drawing his sword and placing himself between the stripling and the other three. "My apologies, but to reach him you must go through me."

They hesitated. Their knives were only a third the length of his weapon. But their numbers lent them courage, and at a gesture from their leader, they spread out to come at him from three sides.

Alain laughed. He lived for moments like this. For the excitement. For the quickening of his pulse and the tingle that shot down his spine. Adopting a guard stance, he held himself still, as if waiting for them to make the first move. It was a ruse, a ploy to have them think he was content to let them take the initiative when nothing could be further from the truth. As his old fencing master had stressed time and again, a defensive strategy was no substitute for a thrust through the heart.

So now, as the trio smirked and warily edged forward, Alain did what they did not expect: He attacked. He thrust at the man in front of him, but it was only a feint. Balanced on the balls of his feet, he swung to the right to meet the rush of another foe, whose knife was poised for a fatal stab. His sword flashed and the man's jugular gushed scarlet. Still in motion, Alain shifted again and thrust at the stomach of the big one. He thought to bury his sword to the hilt but the big one's reflexes were exceptional; the man sidestepped and skipped out of range.

The one Alain had just slashed was on the ground, thrashing and blubbering, his chest bright red.

"Damn you!" the big one spat, and added a string of obscenities. "I'll gut you like a fish."

"Others have tried, monsieur, and failed," Alain said. "I am not without some small skill as a swordsman." To demonstrate, he launched into a flurry intended to overwhelm his adversary by pure finesse. His parries were superbly executed, his ripostes streaks of lightning.

The footpad tried to stave off the inevitable, but he was clumsy in comparison, his mastery of the knife nowhere near the level of Alain's mastery of the sword. Forced back against a wall, the man froze when the sharp tip of Alain's blade was pressed to his throat.

"Any last comments, monsieur?"

"Just one," the ruffian said, and grinned. "It's too bad you don't have eyes in the back of your head."

Alain tried to turn. He had neglected to keep track of the others and paid for his blunder with a blow to the back of his head that dropped him to his hands and knees. He retained his grip on his sword but the world spun like a child's top and it was all he could do to form a coherent thought.

"Now you die, Creole!"

Alain lunged out of blind instinct and felt his blade shear through cloth and flesh. There was a gurgling grunt, then a wet sucking sound as he yanked his sword out. The thud of a body proved his thrust had been true. But his elation was short lived.

"Bastard!"

A boot slammed into Alain's ribs. He doubled over, fighting excruciating waves of pain. His wrist was seized and twisted, and try though he might to hold on, the sword was wrested from his grasp. Another kick, between his legs, pitched him onto his stomach. Bitter bile rose in his gorge, and blinking, he glanced up to see the leader about to skewer him with his own weapon.

"I will enjoy killing you."

The thunk of the bowie knife imbedding itself in the big man's chest surprised them both. The man gaped at the hilt. His mouth moved, but no words came out. Then, like a puppet shorn of the strings that held it up, the big footpad crumpled, exhaled, and was still.

Alain lowered his forehead to the ground and sucked air deep into his lungs. Gradually his head cleared to where he could stand to thank his savior. Much to his amazement, the half-breed was nowhere to be seen. The stripling had pulled out the bowie and left without making so much as a whisper of sound.

*"Mon Dieu!"* Alain exclaimed, impressed. Of the seven bodies sprawled in the throes of violent death, the young man had accounted for four. *"Formidable!"* He scanned the street but it was empty. Reclaiming his sword, he hastened toward the waterfront. The night was still young and there was a certain tavern wench who would be devastated if she were deprived of his company.

Bubbling with a zest for life denied most others, Alain de Fortier laughed.

# Chapter Two

Started by the French, later ceded to the Spanish, and now under American control thanks to Thomas Jefferson's master stroke, the Louisiana Purchase, New Orleans was the fastest-growing city in the United States. With a population of more than one hundred thousand, the port was a cosmopolitan mix of many nationalities and cultures, a thriving beehive of avarice and promise.

Its coffers swelled in large part thanks to two industries. Shipping, primarily cotton, was the city's financial mainstay. More than two thousand steamboats plied the Mississippi River and its tributaries, bearing cotton as well as trade goods, and a two-legged commodity: People flocked to New Orleans from all over. Tourism, the second mainstay, was booming, due to the city's justly deserved reputation for culture and opulence.

11

Less talked about, at least in polite society, was another of its reputations—that of decadence. It was whispered that in New Orleans, "Anything goes!", and it was literally true. Anything anyone could think of, any vice, any desire, any passion, was there for the taking—for a price.

The streets bordering the docks were lined with taverns and bars, flophouses and clip joints. Gaudy houses of ill repute were more numerous than the cats on the city's wharves.

It was through this very section of the city that Zachary King briskly made his way, grim and determined. He had shut the incident with the Creole and the footpads from his mind seconds after it was over. For him, a child of the mountains and the plains, a man who had fought Blackfeet and Sioux and battled a giant grizzly to the death, the fight was a small event, worthy of little note. Especially when he had something much more important on his mind.

Zach was hunting a certain establishment. He had a name, and knew the street, but not the exact street number. Around him swirled a surging stream of humanity: a polyglot mix of French and Spanish extraction, Americans born and bred, and immigrants from Germany, Italy and elsewhere. Choctaw Indians were conspicuous by their dress and aloofness. Many blacks were also in evidence, and many of them free, not slaves.

There were far too many of all kinds for Zach's liking. He had been raised in the wilderness where a man could ride for days, even weeks, without seeing another soul, and he much preferred the solitude to having so many strangers brushing his elbows. Give him the vast open spaces, the mountains and the plains, any day. This made his skin crawl. It was akin to being overrun by fleas, the sensation he felt, only worse.

Suddenly someone bumped into him, jarring him, and Zach's hand automatically dropped to his bowie. But it was only a white-haired old man who smiled and said, "My utmost apologies, young sir. I wasn't paying attention to where I was going."

"Be careful," Zach said gruffly, and stalked on, but he had only taken a few long strides when he thought to slip a hand up under his shirt and ensure his poke was tied in place. Pickpockets were epidemic, and were so skilled at their craft it was said they could swipe a purse or poke without the bearer feeling a thing. Let one try to take mine, he reflected, and he'll be missing his fingers.

The next corner was lit by a street lamp. It was River Street, the one Zach was searching for. "One of the most dangerous places in the whole damn city," the crewman who gave him the address had said. "Be careful, boy. There are wolves abroad, and they have two legs, not four."

Zach had thanked the Irishman and hurried off. Every minute was crucial. He must find the person he was looking for before his real quarry departed the city, taking with her any chance he had of saving one who meant more to him than life itself. He turned right, or started to, and fingers fell on his shoulder. Again his hand dropped to his bowie, and he spun. It was a woman.

"Well, hello, handsome. Are you an Indian? No, you can't be, not with those lovely blue eyes of yours." She was young and pretty, with an oval chin and a button nose. She had marvelous hazel eyes, worldly wise and weary eyes that hinted at experiences no woman should have. A cheap dress clung to her slouched body, and the scent of lilacs wreathed her brown hair.

"Men are not lovely," Zach said curtly, and turned to go. But she held on to his arm and stepped up close so that her bosom brushed his arm.

"Hold on there. What's your rush? How about treating a girl to a drink? Afterward, if you're real nice, and have five dollars, you can get lucky."

"If you mean what I think you mean, I am married." Once more Zach tried to continue on his way but she pulled on his sleeve.

"Dang, you're a strange one. What does having a wife have to do with anything? Hell, most married men leap at the chance."

"Not me," Zach said, and tugging loose, he hurried off. He thought that would be the end of it, but to his considerable consternation she stuck to him like a she-bear drawn to honey.

"Can't you stand still for two seconds? How is a girl supposed to have a conversation with you?"

"Go pester someone else," Zach said. He did not need this, he did not need this at all.

14

The woman, amazingly enough, laughed. "Oh, you don't mean that. I might not be as grand as the ladies at the St. Charles, but no one refuses Apple Annie. No sir."

The words were out of Zach's mouth before he could stop them. "Apple Annie? What kind of name is that?"

"Hey, now. Be polite. I'm called Apple Annie because during the day I sell apples. And my given name is Ann. Ann Webster. Annabelle Clarice Webster, if you must know. I was named after my great-grandmother because I was the oldest, and my sister, she was named after my grandmother because—"

Zach stopped and faced her. Taking hold of her shoulders, he looked her in the eyes. "Go inflict yourself on someone else, you silly woman. I am busy." He gave her a slight shake and wheeled, confident that now she would take the hint. But hardly had he taken two steps when there she was at his side.

"'Inflict.' I like that. You don't hear folks use that much. You must be a reader, like me. Well, like I was, anyway, before my father lost every cent we had and—"

Once again Zach cut her off by grabbing her by the arms. "Is there a brain between those ears? I do not want to talk to you. I do not want your company. I do not want to see you ever again. Do you understand?"

"Yes," Apple Annie said.

"Good." Zach pushed her and continued up River Street, and damned if she wasn't glued to his side and grinning idiotically.

"Has anyone ever told you that your lower lip twitches when you're mad?" Annie asked. "That is so cute."

"If I shoot you, will you leave me alone?"

"With what? Your bowie? You're not carrying a pistol. I can tell." Annie chortled. "And you called me silly."

Zach had heard that more murders were committed in New Orleans than any other city. He was beginning to understand why. As for his guns, he had not liked leaving them with his other effects but it was forbidden to wear firearms within the city limits. Which was why nearly every man carried a knife or sword.

"You haven't told me your name yet. What is it? And what are you up to? Anything I can help you with? It's as plain as those beaded buckskins you're new here." Apple Annie chattered away.

His annoyance mounting, Zach halted one last time. "Do you do this to everyone?"

"Do what?"

"Impose yourself. Latch on to them like a mink on to a fish and not give them a second's peace?" Zach raised his voice. "Go away! I mean it! I will not warn you again!" This time he took four steps before she caught up.

"A mink on to a fish? I've never heard that expression before. Is that one they use where you come from? Where is that, anyhow? I bet you're Canadian. I hear they're the moodiest people on God's green earth. Why—"

Zach slapped her. Not hard—but enough to sting. Then he turned his back to her and bent his steps toward a brightly lit four-story house. The crewman had told him the place would stand out like a bonfire, so maybe this was it.

"That hurt, you know."

Zach had not heard her come up behind him. Furious, he spun. He balled his fists, then saw a tear trickling down her reddened cheek. "Damn you."

"Is that any way to talk to a lady? What would your wife say?"

"Don't you dare bring her up!" Zach missed Louisa so much it hurt whenever he thought of her. But he had done the right thing in sneaking out on her. He was utterly convinced of that.

"Why not? Are you embarrassed she's your wife? If you ask me, and you haven't, a man should be grateful when a woman agrees to put up with him for the rest of her natural-born days. Half the men I know, you couldn't pay me to live with them."

"Money? Is that what this is about?" Zach pulled out his poke, undid the tie, and fished out a coin. "Here. Take it and go."

"One whole dollar, huh? Sure you can spare it?" Annie dropped the coin into his palm. "Keep it. Maybe you can save enough to buy yourself a new disposition."

"Five dollars," Zach said, adding more coins. "It's half of all I have."

"For real?" Annie gave him an odd look, then grinned and brazenly slipped an arm through his. "Where are we off to? I hope someplace that serves food. I'm starved."

"Fifteen dollars?" At this point Zach figured it would be money well spent. "That's as much as I can give."

"I don't want your money. All I want is your company for a while. Is that too much to ask?"

"Why me?"

"Why not?" Annie squeezed him. "Truth to tell, I'm lonely and I'm bored and I can use a friend and there's something about you that interests me."

"Annie," Zach said, prying her loose, "I am sorry, but I have no time for this. Someone I care for is in great danger." He pressed the coins into her hand and left before she could think to stop him. When he glanced back, she was standing there staring at the money.

Sighing in relief, Zach came to the well-lit house. Whiskers and Tails was exactly as the crewman had described it: ablaze with light, four stories high, an old and once stately house converted to pleasurable pursuits. From within came gay laughter and the babble of many voices. Men and women dressed in the most expensive height of fashion were visible through windows on every floor.

Zach bounded up the broad marble stairs, past a row of large columns. He was almost to the door when two men in smart jackets and shirts materialized out of the shadows. Both were big, brawny and black.

"May we help you, sir?" politely asked the one on the right, the older of the pair.

"I need to see Captain Massey," Zach said.

The black on the left smiled courteously. "We're sorry, sir, but this is a private club. Only members are admitted." He paused and looked Zach up and down. "Are you perhaps a member, sir?"

"No. But it's important," Zach informed them, and extended a hand to the silver embossed latch. "Step aside."

Instead, they stood shoulder to shoulder, effectively barring his way, and the older black said, not unkindly, "We would be remiss in our duties, sir, if we permitted you to enter."

"You don't understand." Zach had half a mind to fight his way in. He had to remind himself these were only servants doing their job.

"Please, sir. Be a good gentleman and leave," said the younger one. "We do not want to make you go."

"I *must* see him," Zach stressed, and then he had a brainstorm. "How about if one of you does me a favor?"

"A favor, sir?" said the older black. He was graying at the temples and had a reserved dignity about him.

"Take a message to Captain Massey for me. Tell him it's urgent I speak to him. A matter of life and death."

They glanced at one another and the older black said, "I will check with our mistress and if she gives her consent, we will do as you ask." He went in.

"Your mistress?" Zach said.

"Miss Kitanzia Dyakonov, sir," said the young black. "Everyone calls her Miss Kitty. This is her establishment. A more elegant and gracious lady you could never hope to meet." He opened the door. "She bought my father and me over a year ago and set us free the very next day."

A couple wearing clothes that cost more than Zach had earned in his whole lifetime came strolling merrily up the stairs and the servant moved aside so they could enter. They stared at Zach. The woman tittered and her wealthy escort joked to the young black, "What's this, James? Is it a costume night and no one told us?"

"No sir, Mr. Piedmont, sir," James dutifully said, and admitted them. In the awkward silence that followed, he commented, "Don't take what he said personal. His kind always look down their noses at our kind."

"At blacks and breeds, you mean?"

"At poor folk," James said. "Those who have money generally think that makes them better than those who don't."

"Then why do you work here?" Zach wondered. He had too much pride to abide anyone who thought he was inferior.

"Out of respect for Kitty and the kindness she did us in setting us free. It cost her close to five thousands dollars for us and our families, and she has never asked us to repay a cent. She got us these jobs, she pays us a salary. My pa and me will work for her until the day we die." James studied him. "What do you do, if you don't mind my asking, sir?"

"Call me Zach, not 'sir.' I hunt, I fish, I do some trapping. There's little demand for beaver plews these days but other hides fetch a fair price. Griz skins, for one. I hear folks make rugs out of them."

"You're a frontiersman?" James asked, sounding impressed.

"Some call us that. Others have taken to calling us mountain men." Personally, Zach liked the name the early trappers used: mountaineers.

More patrons of Whiskers and Tails came up the stairs and James let them by. Zach impatiently paced, anxious for word he could go in.

"You sure are a bundle of nerves, sir," James remarked.

"I reckon so," Zach admitted. "But you would be too, if it were your sister's life at stake."

The door opened and out stepped the father. One glance at his expression and Zach knew what the answer had been.

"I am most sorry, sir, but Kitty does not wish Captain Massey to be disturbed. I am afraid you must leave."

Like hell, Zach thought, and stood his ground. Whether they liked it or not, whether their mistress liked it or not, he was going in, and no one would stop him.

# Chapter Three

The fence was seven feet high but all Zach had to do was take a few steps back to get a running start, leap with his arms outstretched, catch hold, and swing himself over. He landed lightly on the balls of his feet and crouched in the darkness, his right hand on his knife.

Enough light spilled from the windows to reveal a wide yard, neatly trimmed flower gardens, and a footpath leading to a short flight of steps and the back door.

Zach started forward but instantly froze when a low, menacing growl emanated from a far corner. A shadow detached itself from the mantle of night; a four-legged form that slunk slowly toward him, its bared teeth a slash of white against the black of its hide. Blazing like red coals, the guard dog's eyes reflected the lamp light from inside.

Zach didn't need to confront it. He had plenty of time to turn and swing back over the fence before the dog could reach him. But he held his ground. The stakes were too high, time too precious, for him to turn tail, no matter how big and threatening the dog might be.

And it *was* big. As large as a mountain lion but with a stub tail and a longer head and jaws. Jaws rimmed with razor teeth that glistened all the more brightly as the space between them narrowed.

The dog had its belly low to the ground and was stalking him with the slow determination of a wolverine. Raising its muzzle into the breeze, it sniffed a few times to read his scent. Another growl rumbled from its chest.

Suddenly straightening, Zach boldly walked toward the house, saying sternly, "Sit, boy! Sit!" He thought that maybe, just maybe, the dog would heed the authority in his tone and obey. But some gambles did not pay off and this was one. He had only taken a couple of steps when the dog snarled and came at him like a wolf gone rabid.

There was a streak of black and the dog's powerful jaws gnashed and snapped as it sought to rip Zach's legs out from under him. Only Zach wasn't there. At the last possible instant he leaped straight into the air, his legs tucked to his chest. The dog bounded under him, abruptly stopped, and whirled just as Zach alighted in a crouch.

For a few moments they were eye-to-eye, the dog's nape bristling, its breath fanning Zach's face.

Zach began to back toward the porch. Just like that, the dog was on the attack. It sprang at his neck, at his jugular, and would have ripped his flesh open had he not met it with a lightning slash of his bowie. Blood spurted, and the dog yipped and twisted and landed to one side, coiled for another spring.

Risking a glance at the windows, Zach made sure no one was looking out. The momentary distraction proved costly, though, because in the fleeting instant his eyes were off the dog, it leapt and fastened its jaw onto his left wrist.

Excruciating pain lanced up Zach's arm, jangling every nerve in his whipcord-tough body. Twisting his forearm, he wrenched for all he was worth. He only had heartbeats before the dog's saber teeth sheared clean to the bone.

With a ripping of buckskin and a rending of flesh, Zach tore his arm free and backpedaled. Moistness spread down his wrist as he crouched to meet the dog's next charge.

Snarling viciously, the animal came in low and fast. It went for Zach's legs this time and he narrowly avoided having them bowled out from under him. Zach swung and missed. The dog had veered wide. Wheeling, it coiled, then jumped, arcing high.

Zach did not duck or dodge; he met the beast head-on with a stroke that would cleave a sapling. The bowie's heavy blade sheared through hide and sinew like a hot knife through wax.

Yipping, the dog scrabbled away and stood with its legs splayed wide as a scarlet torrent soaked the grass. It opened its mouth to bark and more blood spewed from its mouth and nose. Gagging, it tottered toward the house but only went a short way when its front legs folded and it pitched onto its chest.

Zach straightened and checked the windows again. When he lowered his gaze the dog was on its side, its legs thrashing and jerking spasmodically. He thought of the pet wolf he once had and a twinge of regret stabbed through him. But only a twinge, which he shrugged off as he moved to the steps.

A sharp pang prompted him to examine his wrist. A six-inch rent in the sleeve would need mending. One of the dog's canines had left a furrow in his skin almost as long, but it was not deep and was barely bleeding. Dressing it could wait. He had been hurt a lot worse. Compared to some wounds he had suffered, this was a trifle.

Hunkering, Zach wiped the bowie's dripping blade clean on the grass and replaced it in its beaded sheath made for him by his mother years ago, before he took a wife. His moccasins made no noise on the steps, nor as he crossed to the door. He was mildly surprised to find it unlocked.

Zack poked his head in, then immediately drew it back again. The door opened into a wide hallway brightly lit by lamps and filled with people moving to and fro; men in expensive frock coats with checked or striped trousers and vests, women in flowing silk dresses. He would stand out like a buffalo in a horse herd, and the last thing he wanted was to attract attention. He *must* find Captain Massey.

There was a sound to Zach's left. He flattened as another door thirty feet away opened, a door he had not noticed. From it stepped an Hispanic man dressed all in white, including a white apron. Cheerfully whistling, he walked to a stack of chopped wood, helped himself to half a dozen logs, and went back inside, pulling the door shut after him with his toe.

The night was warm. Zach could not think of why they would want a fire until he had moved close to the other door and smelled the mouth-watering aroma of roast beef. He cracked the door and discovered a short hall that led into a kitchen. Other staff in white were bustling about preparing meals and cakes and pies.

Crossing it unnoticed would be impossible. Then Zach noticed several white jackets and pants on pegs near the door. He selected the largest and pulled them on over his buckskins. The pants had a tie, the jacket a string of buttons. It was not much of a disguise but it would have to do.

Zach waited until most of the kitchen workers had their backs to him, then made a swift beeline for a door on the other side. He was almost there when someone called out, "Hey there! Who are you?" Before anyone could stop him, he was through and hurrying along a crowded hall, his chin tucked to his chest. He reasoned that no one would pay much attention to him and assume he was one of the hired help.

Finding the steamboat captain proved difficult. The house had dozens of rooms and each was jammed. The crewman had told Zach that Whiskers and Tails was one of the most popular night spots in all of New Orleans, and he hadn't exaggerated.

Everyone was having a grand time. Couples embraced, fondled, snuggled and kissed. Others were talking, joking, laughing. In some rooms, darker than the rest, more intimate touching took place. In other rooms, brightly illuminated by chandeliers, various games of chance were popular.

A winding flight of polished teak stairs took Zach to the second floor. The rails were gleaming brass, the walls adorned with paintings. To say the place was opulent was an understatement. Plush carpet covered the floors, and the glass lamps were trimmed with gold.

Zach noticed the luxuries only in passing as he moved from room to room. The next was more spacious than most and at the center was a large circular table at which sat eight men and two women engrossed in cards. He gave them a cursory glance and was turning away when a comment fell on his ears.

"How much longer will you keep us waiting, Massey?"

The table was ringed by so many spectators that Zach had not noticed a heavyset man in a blue jacket and blue cap over by a bar. Bushy sideburns and thick jowels further fit the description Zach had been given. At the moment, the steamboat captain had a buxom woman in each arm and was whispering into the ear of one while the other nibbled on his lobe.

"Did you hear me?" the annoyed player demanded.

"Yes, yes, a thousand times yes," Captain Massey responded wearily. "I do declare, Vasklin, that you have no sense of decorum."

"Says the one who has kept us waiting over five minutes while he trifles with a pair of tarts," responded Vasklin, a short, swarthy man with greasy black hair and a greasy, pencil-thin mustache.

Sighing, Captain Massey patted the women on their fannies and ambled to an empty chair at the table. "Have you no romance in your soul? I was arranging a rendezvous for later."

"Arrange them on your own time, not ours," was the indignant reply.

Captain Massey glared and jabbed a thick finger at his accuser, about to offer a strong retort, when another player, a tall, broad-shouldered, handsome man in a fine black frock coat superbly chiseled to his powerful frame, leaned forward.

"I would suggest that is quite enough out of both of you. We are here to play poker, gentlemen. Let's play it."

His words were uttered softly, yet the effect on the captain and Vasklin was remarkable. Both sat back, and Captain Massey said much too hastily, "Certainly, Duncan. Whatever you say."

"That is *Mister* Duncan to you," said the man in the frock coat. "And I believe, Captain, it is your turn to call or fold."

Zach threaded in among the onlookers and worked his way around the table. A lovely blond across from Duncan fluttered a fan and teasingly asked, "Are all professional gamblers so serious about their card playing?"

"To you, Miss Stevens, this is no more than an hour's diversion," Duncan responded suavely. "To me it is my livelihood. So yes, indeed, I take breaches of etiquette quite seriously, thank you."

Vasklin smiled thinly. "Serious enough to kill four men in duels over alleged cheating, eh?"

Duncan's penetrating gray eyes shifted to the swarthy player. "Are you claiming I lied about your brother dealing from the bottom of the deck?"

All conversation ceased. Everyone stared expectantly at Vasklin. Those nearest to him cleared a space around his chair.

"I would never call you a liar, *Mister* Duncan," Vasklin said with mock civility.

"That's good," Duncan said, "since all the other players at the table that night saw him cheat, as well. We offered him the chance to make good on our losses but he refused. He left me no recourse."

"There was no other way to satisfy your honor?" Vasklin asked with more than a little bitterness. "You know dueling is frowned on by the authorities, and few duels are fought."

"What are you implying?" Duncan demanded.

"Only that perhaps a more civilized means of settling the situation might have been better."

Captain Massey cleared his throat. "Gentlemen, gentlemen, if you please. Your differences on this matter are well known. But now is hardly the proper time or place to air them." He smiled at the gambler in black. "I thought you were eager to resume play?"

By then Zach was behind the captain's chair. Bending over Massey's beefy shoulder, he said, "I need to talk to you."

Massey gave a start and blinked. "I beg your pardon? Is this about my supper? I thought I made my wishes quite explicit."

"It's personal," Zach said, and would have gone on except that Vasklin took exception to the interruption.

"What's this? First we have to twiddle our thumbs waiting for the good captain to indulge his lechery, and now the kitchen help is delaying our game? I swear. The quality of this establishment has taken a definite drop."

From out of the onlookers stepped a ravishing woman whose reddish-brown hair cascaded past her slender shoulders in lustrous wavelets. She wore a floral silk dress exquisite beyond compare. "How is that again, Mr. Vasklin?"

"Kitty!" Vasklin blurted, and shifted uncomfortably. "I didn't mean that literally, of course."

"I hope not, for your sake," Kitanzia Dyakonov said. "The last person to speak ill of my place was banned from setting foot inside for a year." She gave an imperious toss of her curls and fixed Zach with a quizzical glance. "What on earth are you doing up here? The kitchen staff are not ever to leave the kitchen." She paused. "Wait a minute. I don't recall ever seeing you before."

Captain Massey's bushy eyebrows met over his nose. "This fellow doesn't work for you? Then why is he imposing on me?"

"It's personal," Zach said, and tugged on Massey's jacket. "All I need is a minute of your time in private."

"What nerve!" Massey declared. "Unhand me, sir, and go annoy someone else. Can't you see I'm in the middle of a card game?"

"You heard him, boy," Vasklin snapped. "Or should I say *breed*. If not for those blue eyes of yours, I'd have taken you for a savage."

The greasy little man would never know how close he came to having his throat slit. But Zach ignored him and gripped Massey harder. "Please. It's important. I must speak to you."

"Unhand me, I say!" the captain bellowed.

Kitty was moving toward a bright pink cord suspended from the ceiling near the door. "I don't know who you are or what you are up to, but no one badgers my customers and gets away with it." She yanked hard on the cord. "You have exactly sixty seconds to make yourself scarce or I will have you tossed out on your arrogant backside."

"No. You don't understand." Zach started toward her to explain, but Vasklin pushed back his chair, blocking him.

"Didn't you hear the lady, breed?" Rising, Vasklin seized the front of Zach's white jacket. "Why is it your kind always have the manners of a goat?" He moved toward the doorway, hauling Zach after him. "I'll throw you out myself and save Kitty the trouble."

"Let go of me," Zach warned. His patience had its limits.

"Don't threaten me, boy. I have killed men for less." Zach had had enough.

# Chapter Four

Zach had always had a problem with his temper, but in recent years it had grown worse. Time after time it got him into trouble. Time after time he made up his mind never to give in to it again, and time after time he broke his vow.

Now, as the player called Vasklin practically dragged him around the table in full view of the amused spectators, Zach's blood began to roar through his veins and the room and everyone in it acquired a reddish tint, as if he were looking at them through a piece of ruby quartz.

Zach had already asked once to be let go. He did not ask again; he planted an uppercut that sent Vasklin sprawling. Then, turning to Captain Massey, whose cucumber lips were parted in a stupefied O, he beseeched, "All I need is a minute of your time. Please."

"You'll get less than that," Kitty said, and snapped her fingers.

Through the crowd waded four men. Two were James and James's father, and when they saw him, they both slowed, but not the other two.

Rough fingers closed on Zach's arms. His hurt wrist flared anew with pain as he was propelled toward the hallway.

"Unless you're fond of broken bones, make this easy on yourself," said one of those responsible, a burly slab in an ill-fitting suit.

To be so close and then to be denied was more than Zach could bear. With a powerful wrench, he shoved them from him and wheeled one more time toward Captain Massey. "You will talk to me whether you want to or not."

The steamboat skipper chuckled. "I think not, dear boy. Look behind you."

Zach should have known better. He glanced over his shoulder and saw a fist streaking at his face. He tried to sidestep, but the fist connected and stars sparkled before his eyes. Oddly enough, he did not feel much pain, but he did with the next punch, a blow to his gut that doubled him over.

"Get him out of here!" Kitty commanded. "And don't be gentle about it, either, after his antics."

Zach let himself go limp, let them think he was too dazed to resist. Then he whipped his fists up and back while simultaneously spinning toward the table. He broke free, but before he could capitalize, James and

James's father had replaced the pair he knocked aside, each with a firm hold on his wrists.

"Please come along quietly, sir," James urged.

Zach almost drew his bowie. He was so incensed, he would gladly have laid about him right and left, cleaving skulls and slitting throats, but James had treated him decently, and the pair were not to blame for their mistress's actions. Containing himself, he allowed them to take him into the hall. "You can let go now," he said. "I won't fight."

"No, we can't," James replied, and moved faster. To his father he said, "We have to get him out of here before Tilly and Egan get hold of him."

They didn't make it. They were halfway down the stairs when the two Zach had punched caught up and rudely pushed the two blacks away.

"We'll take over from here," declared the huskiest. His suit could not hide the the stamp of low character and innate cruelty on his face.

"You bet your ass we will, Tilly," said the other, who must have been Egan. "We'll show him to the door."

To resist at this point, Zach decided, was foolish. He would wait outside for Captain Massey to leave. He thought Kitty's hirelings would toss him out the front door, but they roughly bore him toward the kitchen, Tilly barking at the staff, "Out of our way! Out of our way!"

Everyone stared. Not that Zach cared. After tonight he would never see them again. He didn't resist as he was ushered through the kitchen to the short hallway beyond. He didn't complain as the white jacket and white pants were stripped off. Nor did he say anything when Egan opened the back door and Tilly shoved him outside. A second or two later the door slammed shut.

Zach assumed that was the end of it. Smoothing his buckskin shirt, he took a step. Too late, he heard the rustle of clothes. Too late, he realized they had followed him out, and he tried to turn, raising his arms to protect himself. A tremendous blow to the back of his skull nearly caved it in. He was vaguely aware of sinking to his knees and of having his hair gripped and his face bent up.

"That's just for starters, boy," Tilly said.

Zach's vision cleared and he saw that both held stout wooden clubs. Where they had obtained them, he couldn't say, unless the clubs were kept near the back door for just such an occasion as this.

"Hit us, will you?" Egan said, and planted his feet.

Zach thrust his left arm above his head and nearly cried out when a club struck with a *thud*. He started to slide back out of reach but Tilly caught him across the ribs, spiking them with fire. Barely conscious, he flung himself toward the fence. A club smashed against his temple. More blows pummeled his shoulders. He heard mocking laughter. Then his cheek smacked the ground and the world faded to nothingness.

The feel of a hand on his brow jolted Zach out of the void. He sat up with a start but only made it halfway before an avalanche of horrendous torment slammed through him. Everything spun, inside and out, and he collapsed on his back and bit back a budding groan.

"That will teach you," someone said. "They pounded on you something awful. It's best if you just lie there."

Cracking his eyelids, Zach struggled to make sense of all the swirling hues and shapes. Gradually they acquired forms he recognized. "You?" he croaked, his head echoing with thunder.

"Yes, me," Apple Annie said, smiling. "I saw them beat you and throw you in the alley. What did you do to make them so mad?"

"Go away."

"I do that and you might not make it through the night," Annie said. "Or don't you know that they nearly busted your brainpan?"

She exaggerated, but not by much. Zach's questing fingers found a deep gash wet with blood. Again he attempted to sit but dizziness drove him back down. His stomach did flip-flops.

"You're not much for taking advice, are you?" Annie scolded. "But I shouldn't blame you. All men are as pigheaded as mules." She pursed her lips. "Or should that be as muleheaded as pigs?"

"You are touched in the head," Zach said weakly. His tongue felt thick and sluggish, and it required all his concentration to speak.

Apple Annie snickered. "You dare call me crazy after the stunt you just pulled? You've made an enemy of one of the most powerful ladies in the whole city. Her, and whoever else was in there." Annie nervously glanced up. "Now that I think about it, maybe we should make ourselves scarce before those two bruisers take it into their noggins to finish what they started."

A hand slipped gently under his shoulders and she raised Zach high enough for him to sit up. Mumbling his thanks, he placed his palms flat on the ground to push to his feet. "I can manage on my own now."

"You're plumb ridiculous, do you know that? The shape you're in, you couldn't lick a drowned puppy. Put your arm around my shoulder, like so, and your other hand on my hip, like that, and we'll see about making it to my place without you keeling over."

In the throes of despair, Zach said, "But Evelyn—"

"Who's she? Your wife? Your girl? Wouldn't you know it." Grunting from the strain, Annie moved off down the alley. "Why are all the cute ones always spoken for?"

"No, no, Lou," Zach sought to make things clear, but his muddied brain was a maze of confusion.

"You've got two women?" Annie said something he could not quite catch. "Crushed hopes twice over. Thanks a lot." She shifted to better bear his weight. "Lordy, you must be solid muscle. Has to be all that moose milk you drink."

Zach wanted to tell her that he had never seen a moose, much less drunk from a female moose's teat, but his vocal cords would not work.

"I can't wait to hear about life on the frontier. I've always had a hankering to go there, but with all the talk of hostile redskins and wild animals that would as soon eat you as sniff you, I figure I'm safer sticking with what I know."

Zach dearly wished she would shut up.

"I have a cousin in California. She went there with her husband, who is in dry goods. She wrote me once. Said the climate is so heavenly, they only have cold weather a few days out of the year. Even in December it's mostly sunny and warm. Or so she claims, but she always was a terrible liar."

"Please," Zach said.

"Please what?" Annie asked. "I can't give you water or bandage you until we reach my apartment. So if you'd like to help instead of plodding along like your feet are turtles, I'd be grateful as a parson on Sunday."

Zach wondered if she had been hit on the head, too. Then, for he knew not how long, he was oblivious to everything except the mechanical movement of his legs and the ceaseless drone of her voice. He seemed to be suspended in foggy ether, never fully aware, never fully unconscious. That changed, though, when he felt her ease him onto his back. She mentioned a bed, and that was the last he heard until a persistent humming woke him up.

Zach lay still, collecting his thoughts and taking stock. His head hurt worse than he could ever remember it hurting and was pounding so hard he could scarcely think. His mouth was so dry that when he moved his tongue to lick his lips, he could not form the spittle to do it. Somewhere nearby Apple Annie was doing the humming. "Must you?" he croaked, and opened his eyes.

Annie was in a rocking chair, knitting. She stopped clacking the needles and bestowed a warm smile. "Well, look who is finally awake. The grump is back among the world of the living."

Zach was on a small bed, covered by a wonderfully soft quilt. The room was barely big enough for the bed and the chair and was as plain as the woman who called it home. "I could use some water."

"And I could use a million dollars," Annie quipped. But she got up and set the knitting in the rocking chair and disappeared into another room, saying, "Don't do any somersaults while I'm gone, you hear?"

Bracing his elbows, Zach sought to rise. He would show her he wasn't a helpless invalid. Then a wave of dizziness and nausea collapsed him flat on his back again. "Damn it all," he chafed at his weakness. This was the last thing he needed. He was losing more precious time.

A shaft of warm sunlight on his cheek drew Zach's gaze to a slit of a window high in the wall. Judging by the position of the sun it was early morning. A whole night had been wasted.

Annie was not gone long. She pulled the rocking chair close to the bed and held his head in her hand while carefully tilting the glass so he could drink. "Take slow sips for starters," she cautioned. "Too much too fast and you'll get sick. Three days without food and water weakens the constitution."

"Three days!" Zach blurted, and broke into a coughing spasm. "That can't be! How could I have been out so long?"

"You're lucky you weren't out permanent."

Zach reached up and touched the bandage she had applied. She had done a good job, and he said so.

"Thanks. I worked at the hospital for a spell a few years ago. Guess I haven't forgotten everything." Annie held the glass to his lips and when he had swallowed, she touched his brow. "I was worried that you were coming down with a fever there for a while."

"I must find Captain Massey," Zach said.

"You're not going anywhere for a while, handsome. What's the big hurry, anyway? Does he owe you money or something?"

"He might have information that will help me find my sister." Zach wearily closed his eyes. He had no energy, no vitality, whatsoever.

"Your sis is missing?" Annie asked.

Zach inadvertently nodded and had to grit his teeth against the throbbing pangs that spiked his cranium. "Her name is Evelyn. She was kidnapped."

Annie paused in the act of raising the glass. "No fooling? Who would do such a thing? And why? How old is this sister of yours? Why aren't your parents here to lend a hand? Are the two of you orphans like me?"

"You ask too many questions."

"How else does a person learn things?" Annie retorted. "What makes you think your sister is in New Orleans? And how does Massey figure into this? Is he the one who took her?"

"No. Evelyn was taken by a woman named Athena Borke. Have you ever heard of her?"

"Can't say as I have, no."

"She is rich, vicious, and out for my blood." Zach sipped more water, relishing the coolness it brought to his parched throat.

"What did you do to get her so mad?"

"I killed her two brothers."

Annie digested this in silence. "I trust you had good cause. I mean, I wouldn't want to think you're one of those fellas who go around killing people for the fun of it."

"Only when necessary," Zach said.

"So let me see if I have this straight. You figure that this Borke woman and your sister were passengers on Captain Massey's steamboat?"

"I know they were. I was hoping Massey might know where they went to after they arrived. A member of his crew told me Massey spent a lot of time in their company on the trip here."

"What is this Athena Borke up to? If she hates you, why abduct your sister? What does she want with Evelyn?"

"I shudder to think," Zach said.

# **Chapter Five**

"Men have boulders between their ears," Apple Annie complained, stretching her winsome legs to match his long strides.

"Go back," Zach said. "I can do this myself."

"Sure you can," she replied tartly. "It's only been a day. You should stay in bed a week, if not more."

Zach ignored her, hoping that would shut her up, and concentrated on clamping a mental lid on the incessant pounding in his head. *Pound, pound, pound,* second after second, minute after minute, hour after hour. It would not stop. Annie had tried to get him to see a doctor but he'd refused. For one thing, he did not have much money left. For another, he was no weakling, to run to a physician over every discomfort. He was a man. More than that, he was a Shoshone warrior, and warriors endured pain without complaint. But damn, it hurt.

"I have half a mind to fetch a sawbones whether you like it or not," Annie threatened.

"And I have half a mind to throw you over my knee and spank you," Zach gruffly replied. As much as he appreciated her kindness, she was one of the most aggravating persons he'd ever met. So unlike his wife, as day was from night. Louisa was always quiet; Annie couldn't stop flapping her gums if her life were at stake. Lou could sit still for hours, thinking or reading. Annie couldn't sit still for two seconds. Lou was everything he ever desired in a woman. Annie was everything that made him want to throw her off a cliff.

"Oh, would you?" she teased, rubbing her shoulder against his. "I haven't been spanked in so long, I've almost forgotten how much fun it is."

"You are a shameless hussy," Zach said bluntly.

"I have as much shame as the next gal. I just hide it better." Annie giggled and hooked her arm around his.

"What do you think you're doing?"

"Pretending you're my beau. I haven't had a beau in ages. Most men don't want to have anything to do with a woman who sells her breasts to anyone with the money."

"I wonder why," Zach said dryly. "And as I keep reminding you, I have a wife. A wife I love very much. I cannot be your beau. The most we can be is friends." He knew it was a mistake the instant the words were out of his mouth.

Annie squealed in delight and pecked his cheek. "Friends it is! You can count on me! Anything you want, just ask."

"What if I ask you to go away?"

"Ha. Funny man. What sort of friend would I be if I let you traipse around New Orleans in the condition you're in?" Annie pressed her cheek to his arm. "The least you could have done was keep the bandage on. So now where you go, I go."

"Is it illegal here to strangle someone?"

Apple Annie sighed. "Has anyone ever mentioned you have a violent nature? I swear, the way you talk, a body would think all you ever want to do is hurt people."

Zach did not say anything. But in his mind he flew back in time to a trading post on the Green River run by a man named Artemis Borke, a devious, greedy no-account who tried to stir up a war between the Shoshones and the Crows. Zach was the one who led the war party that wiped out Borke and the other unscrupulous white traders.

Months later, Borke's brother, Phineas, showed up with an army patrol, intending to have him taken into custody. To lure Zach into the open, Phineas had abducted Louisa. Zach then did what any man worthy of being called a man would do. He killed Phineas and rescued Lou. Only the army didn't quite see things his way, and turned him over to a civilian court to be put on trial.

Zach thought for sure he would be thrown into prison but the jury acquitted him. He had been set to return to the mountains he loved so much when Athena Borke showed up and kidnapped Evelyn as part of her scheme to take revenge for her brothers. He had no idea what Athena had in mind, but it scared him, scared him terribly.

When Zach caught up to them, when he got his hands on Athena Borke, he would do to her as he had done to her siblings, and he would do it without a shred of regret. No one, absolutely *no one*, hurt his family and loved ones and went on living.

The day had started out cloudy but the clouds were dispersing. Sunlight accented the brownish-blue of the water and the white of the raucous birds wheeling above it. The shore was choked with a flotilla of boats of every kind: steamboats, flatboats, Mackinaws, keelboats and rowboats, even a few sailboats used for pleasant diversion by those with money. The humid air was tinged with a fish odor he found most unappealing.

"What's the name of Captain Massey's boat again?" Apple Annie wanted to know.

"The *Betsy Lee*," Zach said. "A stern-wheeler he christened after his daughter." It had taken him three days to locate it. Three days of prowling the docks from before sunrise until long after sunset. Three days of asking everyone he saw. "She's up ahead, just past that side-wheeler." He walked faster, eager to wrest the information from Massey by any means necessary.

"I've been meaning to ask. How much younger is this sister of yours?"

"Nine years," Zach said. Despite the age difference he had always felt close to Evelyn, although when he was younger their constant bickering often made him wish he had a brother instead. Evelyn had always loved to tease him, and to get him into trouble with their parents. His ears still burned whenever he thought of all the times she had tattled on him for doing something of which his folks did not approve.

"That much?" Annie said. "Why, you were nearly full grown when she was still in swaddling diapers."

"Nine is hardly full grown," Zach said. Although he was willing to concede their age difference had added to their many silly misunderstandings.

"When I was nine I was living on the streets and fending for myself," Annie revealed. "I had to learn mighty quick to grow up. It's a wonder I've turned out as pure at heart as I have."

Zach was tempted to mention that he did not think a woman who sold her body could be all that pure, but just then they passed the big side-wheeler and he stopped short in dumbfounded disbelief.

"There's no boat here." Annie stated the obvious, nodding at the empty berth. "Are you sure you have the right spot?"

"Of course I'm sure!" Zach snapped. But he wasn't mad at her. He was mad that fate had thwarted him yet again. He turned to the side-wheeler and hurried to the foot of a gangplank where a variety of goods were being loaded. Half a dozen crewmen regarded him with expressions ranging from amusement to hostility.

"What can we do for you, chief?" one asked at his approach.

"The *Betsy Lee*," Zach said. "Can you tell me how long ago she left? And when she might be back?"

"Why should we?" demanded a crusty river hand with a belly as large as an ale keg.

Another smirked and said, "We'll tell you all you want for a twenty-dollar gold piece."

At that, several laughed. Zach's temper heated, and he was on the verge of drawing his bowie and demanding answers when Apple Annie let go of his arm and pointed at the crewman laughing the loudest. "You're not being very sociable, Jack Webber. Not nearly as sociable as you were the other night when you paid to play around under my skirts."

Webber reddened like a tomato when his friends directed their mirth at him. "You shouldn't bring that up, woman."

"Why not? You certainly enjoyed yourself," Annie said. "Or do you always grunt like a stuck boar in mixed company?"

"You have nerve," Webber said.

Annie sauntered up to him and poked him in the chest. "Why should I be nice to you when you won't be nice to my friend? His sister has been kidnapped, you big oaf, and all he wants is to find her."

"No lie?" Webber responded, and at her emphatic nod, he said to Zach, "Captain Massey took his boat out yesterday morning bound for Fort Union on the upper Missouri. He won't be back for a month of Sundays."

Crestfallen, Zach turned away. Massey had been his best hope of finding Athena Borke, and thus his sister.

"Wait a minute," another man said. "This sister of

yours, does she look a bit like you? Part Indian, I mean, with long dark hair? In the company of a woman about twenty-five to thirty?"

Forgetting himself, Zach ran up and gripped the man's arms. "That might have been them, yes!"

"The only reason I remember is because of the woman," the crewman said. "She could take your breath away, she was so good-looking." He nudged the one with the large belly. "You remember her, Spike. We were unloading a shipment when the *Betsy Lee* put in and her passengers came off. Your eyes about bugged out of your head."

"Oh, her!" the other man exclaimed, and grinned a lecherous grin. "Dang, she made a man drool just to look at her."

Annie put her hands on her hips. "And I don't, I suppose?"

"Begging your pardon, ma'am," the first crewman said. "Sure, you're pretty enough, but this lady was downright gorgeous. Why, the way she walked, it took a fella's breath away. She's the kind of woman that makes a man glad he's a man, if you catch my drift."

"I'd like to catch your head in a vise and squeeze," Annie said. "Or some other part of you lower down."

Zach had no time for her silliness. "Tell me," he said to the pair who had seen Athena Borke and Evelyn, "did you happen to notice which way they went when they left?"

"I can go you one better, chief," Spike said. "They got into a carriage from The Harvest House. You know, the carriage the hotel sends to pick up passengers who have taken rooms in advance."

"Then that clerk lied to me." On Zach's first day in New Orleans, he had spent twelve hours going to every hotel in the city, asking if anyone answering to Athena Borke's description had checked in. The desk clerk at The Harvest House had assured him she wasn't staying there. But now that he thought about it, The Harvest House was one of the two or three most elegant hotels, if not *the* most, and Athena Borke always liked to stay at the best places her more than considerable wealth could afford.

"Hope that helps you," Spike said. "I've got me a sister back in Indiana and I'd hate for anything to happen to her."

Zach thanked them and headed for the heart of the city. "I can go it alone from here."

"There you go again," Annie said. "Friends through thick and thin, remember?" She whistled happily as they strode along. "Besides, I helped you out back there. If not for me they wouldn't have given you the time of day."

"This woman I'm after," Zach made sure to mention, "is as dangerous as a riled bobcat. She's had six people murdered that I know of, and I wouldn't put it past her to do the same to us."

"You're talking to a girl who has had a knife held to her throat by a mad drunk. Who had a wife take shots at her because the husband liked to spend his hours with me instead of at home. A girl who has lived by her wits for so long, it's second nature. This Borke doesn't scare me."

"She should. Your wits won't stop a bullet."

"I can take care of myself," Annie said confidently. "If this Borke gal doesn't turn your sis over, I'll scratch out her eyes and box her ears until she does."

It was something his wife might say, Zach mused, and without meaning to, he patted Annie's arm.

"I've been wanting to ask," Apple Annie said. "Where are you staying? If you don't have a place, I'd be more than happy to put you up for as long as you'd like."

Zach would rather not reveal the truth. Namely, that he couldn't afford a long stay at a hotel or to rent an apartment, so he had staked a claim to a thicket in a strip of woods in the heart of the city. Mothers brought their children there to play in the sun and romantic couples walked hand in hand along the well-trodden paths but no one ever went too near the thorny thickets. His rifle, pistols, ammo pouch and possibles bag were wrapped in a cheap blanket and covered by leaves. Safe enough, he believed, until he needed them.

Annie misconstrued his silence. "No answer, huh? That's all right. I get it. You have the ball and chain to think of."

"She would like you," Zach said. Louisa liked nearly everyone.

"Really?" Annie smiled and smoothed her dress. "Not many women do. It's how I make ends meet that sours them. Not the apple selling, the other."

51

Zach looked at her. "Among some Indian tribes, when a stranger stays the night, if they like the stranger they offer him the company of a woman for the night. Only for the one night, and he is not to take her with him when he goes. But they do not think less of the woman for it."

Annie looked away and her voice became husky. "That was awful kind of you."

"I am not white. I do not see things the way whites do. I am more Shoshone and proud to be so."

"I wish I were part of a tribe. I wish I lived in a village where they didn't look down their noses at me. I wish so many things."

They covered ten blocks in silence. Around them pulsed the lifeblood of the city—waves of pedestrians ebbing to and fro, riders and wagons and carriages rattling and creaking in a tireless testament to human energy, and everywhere the babble of conversation punctuated by laughter and lusty oaths.

From a corner two blocks away, Zach gazed at The Harvest House. It had been painted purple from the ground to the roof. Purple carriages were drawn up in front, each with "The Harvest House" emblazoned in large gold letters on the side.

"How do you aim to go about this?" Annie inquired. "We can't go from room to room demanding everyone open up. I hear they don't let anyone in who doesn't meet their standards."

Before Zach could respond, a doorman in a purple uniform opened a purple-and-gold entrance door and into the afternoon sun walked a shapely woman dressed all in black, her face hidden by a veil that hung from her wide black hat. But it was not the sight of the woman that sent a lightning bolt searing through Zach's chest. It was the downcast girl beside her. "That's Evelyn!"

# Chapter Six

It had been more than a month since Zach King started his desperate search for his sister. More than a month of repeated setbacks, of continual frustration. More than a month of constant, gnawing heartache. Of sleepless nights. Of terrible guilt.

Zach never mentioned it to anyone, but he felt in large measure to blame for his sister's plight. He was the one who'd led the raid on the trading post; he was the one who'd slit Phineas Borke's throat. He was the one Athena Borke hated, and she had taken Evelyn to get back at him, to make him suffer as she had suffered.

Now, setting eyes on Evelyn after so long, Zach's joy and relief were boundless. In his excitement and eagerness to reach her, he dashed into the street without looking. He heard a man yell and glimpsed a wagon bearing down on him, the heavy hooves of the four-horse team pounding the ground like sledgehammers. In his haste he had blundered directly into its path.

Suddenly hands were on the back of his shirt and Apple Annie jerked him to safety with mere seconds to spare. They watched the wagon rumble past, the driver heaping obscenities on Zach's head, and she remarked, "Are you trying to get yourself killed?"

Zach didn't give it a second thought. All he cared about was Evelyn, and rescuing her from Athena Borke's devious clutches. Rising on his toes to see past the traffic, he looked toward the hotel and saw them already in a purple carriage. "No!" he cried, and broke from Annie's grasp to bolt madly toward The Harvest House.

The press of pedestrians hampered him. There were so many they clogged the street, and try as he might, Zach couldn't thread through them fast enough. Frantic, he shouldered aside one sluggard after another, but there were always more. He was still a block from the hotel when the carriage disappeared around a corner.

"Evelyn!" Zach hollered, but she could not hear him above the city's din. His last sight was of her gazing glumly out the window, the portrait of despair. "Evelyn! No!" he groaned, and sagged, racked by sorrow deeper than any he had ever known.

A shadow blotted out the sun. "Are you going to stand there feeling sorry for yourself or are you going to go after her?" Apple Annie pointed.

Nearby was a cab, the driver nibbling on a sweetcake while waiting for fares. Zach sprang to the rear door and quickly climbed in, then offered his arm to Annie.

"Where will it be, sir?" the driver asked, bending to speak through one of the small front windows.

"Catch up to the Harvest House carriage that just pulled out," Zach directed. "Hurry, before we lose them."

"You want me to chase it, sir?" The driver was dubious. "Need I remind you drivers can be fined for reckless driving?"

"There's five dollars in it for you," Zach offered the last of his pittance.

"That much?" The driver flicked his whip. "I'll see what I can do, sir, but I make no promises."

Zach leaned out. The cab had to slow for pedestrians crossing in front of it, and when they reached the corner, the Harvest House carriage was nowhere in sight. A swarm of butterflies filled his stomach and he smacked the door and shouted, "Faster! We can't lose them!"

At the next corner Zach looked both ways but did not spot it. The driver went on to the next, and then the one after that, and on down the thoroughfare until they had gone half a mile without a splash of purple anywhere.

"Do we keep looking, sir?" the driver asked when it was apparent they were chasing thin air.

"Yes" was on the tip of Zach's tongue. He would be damned if he would give up after coming so close.

Annie had a cooler head. "You know, they're bound to return to The Harvest House eventually. It might be smart to be there waiting when they do."

Her idea had merit. "The Harvest House," Zach told the driver, and slid to the edge of the seat, his body as taut as a bowstring, unable to relax even if he'd wanted to. "When we get there you can go back to your place."

"Not that silliness again," Annie said. "Whether you realize it or not, you need my help, and whether you want it or not, you have it."

"Did you see her?" Zach asked. "She looked so sad." It tore him apart inside to think of all Evelyn had been through. All on account of him.

"She's alive, isn't she?" Annie said. "That's what counts." She touched his hand. "Don't worry. By tonight the two of you will be reunited and the Borke woman will be behind bars."

The comment gave Zach a start. He had not told Annie what he planned to do. Athena Borke would not get off that easy. Jail was too good for her. She deserved nothing less than to breathe her last gasp with his knife in her heart.

"What's the matter? You do intend to turn her over to the law, don't you?" Annie asked. When Zach said nothing, she sat back, her eyes widening. "You wouldn't? You *couldn't*!"

"I have killed before," Zach said.

"But a woman? Maybe I could see it if she was pointing at gun at you and you had no choice. But this would be outright murder."

Zach sought to put things in perspective. "On the frontier, people kill other people all the time. White men kill red men. Red men kill white men and other red men. Certain tribes are always at war against other tribes. It is the way of things."

"But a woman?" Annie said.

"When a village is raided, the women defend it as fiercely as the men, and often many die. When the men go on raids, sometimes the women go along, and sometimes they die."

"That's war. It's different. For you to walk up to Athena Borke and blow her brains out is as coldblooded as can be." Annie paused. "I don't think I would like you as much if you did that."

Zach tried a different argument. "She has brought great suffering to my family. Would you have me forgive and forget, as the ministers teach?"

"Why not?" Annie defensively demanded. "What's wrong with turning the other cheek?"

Zach had a story to tell. "When the first missionary came to a rendezvous ten or eleven winters ago, he asked all the Shoshones and Flatheads to gather around. Through an interpreter he talked to them about the white man's religion. He told them all men are brothers and should love one another. He told them that when an enemy walked up to a warrior and slapped him on the cheek, the warrior should turn the other cheek for it to be slapped, as well. I was there. I heard every word. When he was done, the Shoshones and the Flatheads did not say a thing and the missionary went off into his tent."

"What's your point?"

"I'm getting to that. They talked it over around their campfires that night, and they pretty much agreed that while the missionary meant well, he was the dumbest man they ever met."

"The parson was only quoting from Scripture. 'Do unto others as you would have them do unto you.' It's the Golden Rule."

"The *white* Golden Rule," Zach amended. "But whites do not have Bloods and Piegans raiding their villages. Whites do not have Sioux counting coup on them. If all Shoshones lived as that missionary wanted, there wouldn't *be* any Shoshones."

"So you're saying that you don't view killing the way whites view killing?"

Zach nodded.

"But you're part white—"

Zach did not let her finish. "I am also half Shoshone, and long ago I decided to live by the ways of my mother's people and not the ways of my father's. I do not turn the other cheek. I do not extend my hand in friendship to all men and call them my brothers. I do unto others, as you put it, before they do unto me. And once someone has harmed those I care for, I make damn sure they never do it again."

The cab clattered to a stop and the driver leaned down. "We're at the hotel, sir, as you requested."

Fishing out his poke, Zach paid the fare, then made for the golden doors to The Harvest House. They opened, disgorging a doorman in a purple uniform and a purple hat.

"Might I help you, sir?"

"No." Zach tried to go on by, but the doorman shifted. "You're in my way. I'd like to go inside."

"I'm afraid you can't enter the hotel without the permission of the owner, whose instructions in this regard are quite specific. Your kind are not permitted over the threshold."

"My kind?" Zach said, stung by the insult. "This hotel is open to the public, isn't it?"

"Yes, it is," the doorman admitted, "but to a select segment of the public that does not include anyone who is half and half, if you will."

Zach almost hit him. He only refrained because Annie clasped his wrist and stepped between them.

"You can't blame my friend for being upset," she told the doorman. "You would be too if you were him."

"It's not my decision, miss," the doorman said. "I'm only doing what my employer, Mr. Harold Wilkerson, pays me to do. No blacks, no Indians, no half-castes. It's a rule of his."

"But we saw a young girl come out of here a while ago who is part Indian," Annie mentioned. "How does she rate?"

"Are you referring to Miss Evelyn Borke? She looks more white than red. And, too, her aunt, Athena, has been here several times before, and travels in the same social circles as Mr. Wilkerson."

Confusion and shock seized Zach. "What did you just say?"

"Sir?"

60

"Evelyn's last name is King, not Borke, and Athena is no more her aunt than you are."

"I am only repeating what the staff has been told," the doorman said. "Now if you would be so kind, vacate the premises or I will send for a constable."

"What about me?" Apple Annie asked. "Am I allowed inside or is your Mr. Wilkerson only partial to ladies with scads of money?"

"It's all right by me if you go in," the doorman said with a gracious smile, opening the door for her.

Zach yearned to knock him to the ground but Annie turned and pushed on his chest. "Wait for me on the corner. I won't be long. Please. It's for the best." Reluctantly, he backed down the steps and went over to stand beside a parked phaeton where he was less likely to be spotted by Athena Borke if she returned.

Zach was simmering inside. Once again he had been the victim of white bigotry. Everywhere he went, they threw it in his face, a gauntlet he resented with every fiber of his being. And Annie wondered why he had not adopted white ways! For as far back as he could remember, whites had looked down their noses at him because of the color of his skin. Because in their eyes, half of him was somehow inferior to the other half. He was tainted by birth to forever be treated with scorn and prejudice. Nothing he could say, nothing he could do, would ever change that.

It was impossible to stand still so Zach began pacing, his arms folded, his head bowed. To be so close and to be thwarted compounded his anger. Seeing Evelyn had temporarily filled him with joy, but now he was asking the same question he had asked every day since her abduction: To what sinister end had Athena done it? He did not doubt for a second that Athena had something diabolical planned. Her brothers had been as callous as they were vicious, and he had seen nothing to indicate their sister was any different.

Engrossed in his brooding, Zach did not realize a purple carriage had rattled around the corner until it came to a stop near the phaeton. Thinking it might be them, his heart leaped, but the carriage was empty. Hastening over, he forced a smile. "Did you just drop off Athena Borke and a young girl named Evelyn?"

About to climb down, the driver regarded him with a faint air of suspicion. "I did not catch their names, sir."

"A woman in black and a girl of thirteen," Zach clarified. Almost fourteen, now that he thought about it.

"What business might it be of yours?"

Zach resisted grabbing him by his purple coat and dashing him headfirst to the hard ground. Since the driver might not believe him if he said he was Evelyn's brother, he came up with something else. "I have a pony for sale and the woman was interested in buying it. But I got here late and saw them leave."

"Ah." The driver became friendlier. "Yes, you missed them. I dropped them off at the Wilkerson estate."

"Is this the same Wilkerson who owns The Harvest House?"

"One and the same," the driver confirmed. "He's also one of the richest men in the city. Some say *the* richest."

"Then I should go there," Zach said, more to himself.

"I wouldn't, were I you." The driver glanced around, then bent so no one could overhear. "A word of advice. You couldn't set foot on the estate if you wanted to. It's patrolled by guards and dogs twenty-four hours a day."

Zach nodded. "Then I'll wait here for them to return."

"It's my understanding that Miss Borke intends to remain at Mr. Wilkerson's for the remainder of her stay. She's having her effects taken over later." Then the driver said a strange thing. "That poor child."

"How's that?" Zach asked.

"Nothing. Forget I mentioned anything." The driver climbed down and walked to another purple carriage waiting for patrons of the purple hotel to require its services.

A minute later Apple Annie emerged. Her features troubled, she walked slowly, as if dazed, and gave a start when he grabbed her wrist.

"Did they throw you out?"

"It's your sister," Annie said bleakly. "The desk clerk told me they took her to the Wilkerson estate. I've heard tales about that place."

"What kind of tales?" Zach was impatient to be on his way.

"About people who are taken there and never heard from again."

63

# Chapter Seven

The Dark Mansion, it was called. Feared and shunned by the locals. Whispers were spread about strange goings-on at all hours, and of screams and cries occasionally heard in the dead of night.

Harold Wilkerson was notoriously eccentric. Painting his hotel purple was only one example. Another was his mansion, which he had painted completely black. Then he had a ten-foot wall erected and posted guards with dogs to ensure privacy.

Wilkerson was an Easterner who had moved to New Orleans ten years ago from New York City. Little was known about his background other than that he came from an old family of European extraction, and that he had more money than most banks. His name, it was rumored, was not the name the family was known by in

Europe. They had changed it because of dark secrets in the family's past.

Rumor also had it that due to his great wealth and influence, the authorities turned a blind eye to certain unsavory practices in which Harold K. Wilkerson and his select guests indulged.

All this Zach learned on their long walk to the estate. Apple Annie had heard all the stories. About how on certain nights of the year hooded figures could be seen moving about inside the walls, and peculiar chanting was heard. About how Wilkerson dabbled in doings wiser heads avoided. There were whispers of devil worship and arcane rituals.

"A bunch of silliness, if you ask me," was how Zach summed up his sentiments. "Who in their right mind would worship the devil?" Who, in his estimation, did not even exist.

"All I'm doing is repeating what I've heard," Annie said. "It's why no one goes near the Dark Mansion. Ever."

"Then we'll be the first," Zach said, and could not comprehend why she laughed and hugged him.

"You said 'we,'" Annie cooed. "I can't tell you how great it feels to have a friend again."

Zach was going to remark that she was making more of it than she should, but the happy gleam in her eyes changed his mind. She was an odd one, this woman, almost as odd in her way as Harold K. Wilkerson was rumored to be in his. But then, as far as Zach was concerned, the same could be said of most whites. His wife, father, and uncle were rare exceptions.

"Look," Annie suddenly said.

One thing about New Orleans. Much of it was below sea level, the ground so flat, it reminded Zach of the prairie. A person could see for miles when his view wasn't blocked by buildings, and now, standing on a slight hummock in the road, Zach beheld the Wilkerson estate in the distance. It was situated east of the city, in an isolated swampy area, an unusual site for someone to choose to live. High walls surrounded ten acres or more. Beyond, rearing darkly into the overcast afternoon sky, were the black walls and dark roof of the infamous Dark Mansion.

Annie gave a slight shiver even though the temperature had to be in the nineties. "There's something about that place," she said softly, but did not elaborate.

They had walked to spare the expense of a carriage. Zach was low on money, and he refused to impose on Annie's generous nature more than he already had. Now he regretted it. If they had come by carriage he could send her back. For truth to tell, he did not like the looks of the place.

"The Dark Mansion is well named," Annie observed. "I've never been out this far, and I can't say as I ever want to come this way again."

Zach saw that as an opening. "Head back to the city. I'll go on alone from here." A splash in the water diverted his attention to the swamp that hemmed the dirt road on both sides. Shadowy islands of thick vegetation broke its still surface. But there was no life anywhere—no birds taking wing or breaking into song, no insects buzzing or chirping, not even the croak of a frog.

"Like heck you will," Annie said. "When will you stop bringing that up, for goodness sake? I want to do what I can to help your sis."

"You don't know her."

Annie frowned. "That was cruel. I didn't know you, either, but I lent a helping hand when you needed it."

"I'm obliged." But Zach was puzzled by her attachment to him. She knew he was married and nothing could come of it, so why was she being so kind?

"I had a sister," Annie said as though she could read his thoughts. "Winifred. Four years younger than me. When our folks died we were put an in orphanage because my uncle and aunt refused to let us go live with them. The nuns were hoping they could place us a with a family that would take us both but a couple came along and wanted only Winnie." Her fingers strayed to his arm. "I can still see her crying her heart out as they carried her away. It tore me up inside worse than anything."

"I'm sorry," Zach said.

"They said I could write to her and I did but she never wrote back. After about six months I couldn't take it anymore and I slipped out of the orphanage late one night and walked the six miles to the address the nuns had given me. I hid in the bushes waiting for Winnie to show herself but no one ever did. Along about noon an old woman came by and I asked her if she knew where they were and she told me the couple had left about a week after the adoption and she didn't know where they went."

Her voice was breaking so Zach said, "If it hurts you to talk about it, maybe you shouldn't."

"Oh, it's all right. I don't cry about it but once a month or so these days." Annie smiled thinly. "With Winnie gone, I figured I didn't have much to live for so I took to the streets and have been there ever since."

"You're doing all this because my sister makes you think of yours."

Annie averted her face. "Something like that."

Another splash snapped Zach's head around in time to see the tail of a fish flip under the water. Seconds later something else, something much larger, created a swell of ripples that converged on the spot where the fish had disappeared, and the water erupted in a brief frenzy. Then all was still.

"There are gators in the swamp," Annie said. "Some big enough to swallow a person whole, or so people say."

Zach seriously doubted there had ever been an alligator that huge. But he saw something else that brought him to a stop. Guards atop the estate walls were staring in their direction. "We've been spotted," he announced, and instantly wheeled. Darting into the swamp would do no good, and there was nowhere else to hide.

"I wouldn't worry," Annie said. "They don't dare sic their dogs on us. This isn't a private road."

Or was it? Zach wondered. Had Wilkerson paid to have it constructed from his vast fortune? Not that it was of any consequence. The important thing was to avoid arousing suspicion and to get out of there. He would return later, much later, alone, and with his guns.

Annie was gazing over her shoulder. "Your sister has to be in there somewhere. How can we just leave like this?"

"Athena Borke must not suspect I am here," Zach said. His greatest fear now was that she would flee again, taking Evelyn with her.

"How is your head?" Annie unexpectedly asked.

"Fine," Zach lied. It hurt constantly. Any abrupt movement triggered a pounding ache that made thinking difficult.

Thereafter they hiked in silence except for random splashes and furtive rustling from the swamp. Once an enormous snake crossed the road not twenty feet in front of them, its body as thick as Zach's arm, its blunt head triangular, its scaly skin as black as the Dark Mansion.

On they hiked. They neared her apartment. Annie had been glancing at Zach repeatedly as if mustering the nerve to say something. Finally she did. "You're going back tonight, aren't you?"

"Yes."

"Alone?"

Deciding it would serve no purpose to deny it, Zach nodded. He thought she would be mad. He had forgotten how unpredictable females could be. Instead, she chuckled and smacked his shoulder.

"You're a bluff, do you know that? From your too-long hair to the tips of those fancy beaded moccasins, you are one hundred percent bluff."

"Can you speak English or will I need a translator of my own?"

Chortling, Annie said, "You always act so tough, so mean. But deep down inside you're a kitten. I saw through you the first night we met when you gave me that money. You have a heart as big as Louisiana."

Zach remembered the raid on the Borke trading post, remembered the butchered bodies littering the ground afterward, and how in his bloodlust he had slain without mercy. "Think so, do you?"

"I know so. You couldn't harm a fly unless your life depended on it. We're a lot alike, you and me. Two gentle souls trapped in a cold, cruel world."

Of the many ways Zach had been described by many people, "gentle" was not one of them. "I am not as you think I am."

"Sure, sure. That's what all men say. But if you want to pretend you're a mean Shoshone warrior, it's fine by me."

Zach was insulted. He *was* a Shoshone warrior. His mother was Shoshone, and he had spent more time among her people than among whites. He had grown to manhood under the tutelage of renowned Shoshone warriors like Touch The Clouds and Drags The Rope. He had counted coup and was accorded a seat at their councils, a remarkable honor for a half-blood. "There is much of my world you do not know," he settled for saying.

"Just as there is a lot about the white world you don't know," Annie rebutted, "or pretend you don't. But men are good at that, too. Denying what is right in front of their noses."

Her comment made no sense. Taking her hand, Zach shook it. "Here is where we part company. I thank you again for all you have done. Maybe we will meet again in this life."

"You can bet your beads we will," Annie vowed. "I'd like to meet this wife of yours and find out why she took up with someone so loco."

Zach walked off and made it as far as the corner before he had to look back. He was pleased, yet also disappointed, to see she was gone. Inside, no doubt, so she would not break down and cry in front of him. Women were emotional like that. Coughing to clear his throat, he bent his steps to the tract of woodland where his guns were hidden. No one had disturbed them in his absence.

Slinging his possibles bag, powder horn and ammo pouch across his chest and shoulders, Zach verified both his flintlock pistols and his Hawken were loaded, then tucked the pistols under his belt.

Now all he had to do was wait for night to fall.

Stretching out on his back, his hands cupped under his head, Zach closed his eyes. Some rest would do him wonders. All the many sleepless nights, and now the head wound, were taking a toll. He was not as alert as he should be, not the bottomless well of stamina he had always been.

Unbidden, Louisa's image popped into his head. He imagined she was mad enough to beat him with a rock for going off alone as he had and leaving her with his uncle, Shakepseare McNair. For that matter, McNair was bound to be mad, too, because he had lit out without waiting for his father and mother to reach Kansas, where the kidnaping took place.

*Athena Borke.* Zach had seldom loathed anyone as much as he loathed her. He had never desired to hurt a woman before but he keenly desired to hurt her. She did not deserve a quick death, that one. For all the suffering she had caused with her heinous deed, she deserved to be burned alive or to have her skin flayed and then be staked out over an ant hill.

Zach did not try to fool himself about the outcome should he be caught. To whites, harming a woman was unthinkable. Should he be linked to the crime, they would track him down and string him up from the most convenient tree after a not-so-convenient trial. But he would not turn back. He would not change his mind. He was committed to spilling Athena Borke's blood and he would let nothing stand in his way.

Drowsiness came over him, and Zach dozed off. When next he opened his eyes, the sky was dominated by stars. Stunned, he leaped to his feet. The sun had set an hour ago.

Even though it was dark, Zach took the precaution of wrapping the Hawken in his blanket before stepping from the thicket. No one was around, and soon he was bearing east along a side street.

Too few street lamps was a complaint mentioned on the front page of a newspaper Zach had seen. But the *Dispatch*'s pet peeve worked in his favor. He avoided streets that had them. Whenever he came to a house or business with light spilling from its windows, he crossed to the other side. The scores of people he passed remained in complete ignorance of the fact he was armed as if for war.

Beyond the city, the air was pleasantly cool and much less muggy. Once Zach was on the lonely stretch of road to the Wilkerson estate, the night and the swampland closed in around him. The swamp pulsed and throbbed with the croaking of frogs and the chirping of crickets, to say nothing of the many grunts, screeches, cries and snarls that rose in feral chorus.

Zach stuck to the middle of the road. Alligators sometimes came out on land and he would rather not blunder into one in the dark.

Distant bright rectangles gave Zach some idea of how far he had to go. He kept expecting a carriage to come along but none did. When he was within five hundred yards of the high walls, he slowed. He must not be spotted.

Zach was debating whether to slip through the swamp and come up on the estate from the north or the south when a new sound keened as stridently as the shriek of a panther, a sound that momentarily hushed the frogs and crickets and other creatures of the night and formed a ball of gnawing anxiety in the pit of Zach's stomach. There was no mistaking it for anything other than what it was: the scream of a woman, or a young girl, in dire terror.

# Chapter Eight

Zachary King did what most any man would do when he thought someone he loved was in grave peril: He threw precaution to the breeze and flew toward the Wilkerson estate. It was only when he glimpsed movement near the gate and on top of the wall that his folly jarred him like the prick of a dagger and he dug in his heels and slid to a stop, raising swirls of dust.

Crouching, Zach waited for a sharp outcry or some other sign the guards had spotted him. When there was none, he edged to the side of the road. He had almost given himself away, a mistake that could prove fatal for Evelyn. It went without stating that he could not be of any help to her if he were dead.

The challenge now was to get inside without being detected. Since he couldn't very well waltz up to the gate and ask to be admitted, he had to find a way over the high walls. A daunting task, given that he must circle the estate, which was hemmed on three sides by the treacherous swamp.

Zach did not relish the notion of wading into the water. Swamps crawled with snakes, some of them poisonous, and then there were the alligators to consider. It was common knowledge that gators did most of their hunting at night. In the dark, in their element, they were more than a match for any man, no matter how well armed that man might be.

Zach was about to slide his right foot in when a light flared atop the mansion. A torch had been lit. Its glow framed a flat section of roof on which a lone figure stood, a figure clothed in a long flowing robe. As Zach looked on in fascination, the figure raised its arms to the heavens and began chanting. The distance was too great for Zach to catch the words but they did not appear to be English or any other language with which he was familiar.

A shiver rippled down Zach's spine. He recalled Apple Annie's comments about the estate's sinister reputation and the wicked deeds supposedly practiced by its owner. What if the rumors were true? he asked himself. It lent urgency to his need to find his sister and spirit her out of there before something terrible happened to her.

Steeling himself, Zach took a pistol in each hand and held them and his rifle over his head. A chill, clammy, liquid fist closed about his legs and rose as high as his waist as he waded deeper. The frogs went on croaking, the crickets continued to chirp. In the distance rose a bellowing roar that was answered by another, much closer.

Zach's mouth went dry. He licked his lips to moisten them, then moved toward a small island not far from the walls. His leg bumped something that felt like a submerged log but which suddenly swam off, leaving a wake. A little farther, and Zach saw a long, sinuous shape go by on his right. He resisted an impulse to smash it with his Hawken. A mosquito landed on his cheek and he brushed his arm across his face. A soft splash to his left gave him a start but it was only a frog.

Zach had never been so glad to have solid ground under him as he was when he pulled himself onto the island. Rank vegetation choked every square inch, and to reach the other side he had to fight restraining limbs and clinging vines. It would be easier to hack at them with his bowie, but the sound would carry.

Up close, the walls seemed insurmountable. Especially when Zach discovered that all the vegetation within twenty feet of them had been cleared away. He also discovered that the estate had been built on a broad finger of land that jutted into the swamp in a northeasterly direction.

Lying on his stomach in the muck and the slime, Zach debated how best to proceed. Unless there was another gate somewhere, a gate that just happened to be unguarded, his only recourse was to go over the wall. A rope would help but he had not thought to bring one. Stupid, he chided himself.

Zach was about to rise and move on when the scrape of shoes on stone caused him to flatten. A pair of guards were patrolling the top of the wall, bound for the front gate. He could not tell much about them other than they wore dark clothes and were armed with rifles. One made a comment in French, a language Zach was somewhat familiar with from meeting French trappers at the early rendezvous, and from his chance meetings with Canadian voyagers from time to time. But his vocabulary was limited to things like "hello" and "coffee"; he did not understand what the guard was saying.

As soon as the pair was out of earshot, Zach rose, reentered the water, and paralleled the wall. He could not help thinking that under the surface lurked scores of things he could not see—snakes with their wicked curved fangs and alligators with their fearsome rows of bone-shredding teeth.

"The things I do for you, sis," Zach said quietly, and grinned. For all their bickering, for all their many spats, she was his sister and he would do anything for her, including, if need be, giving his life to save hers. They had spent a lot of time together growing up, and he knew that for all her teasing, for all the times she got him into hot water with their folks, as surely as he lived and breathed, she cared for him as deeply as he cared for her.

Zach sometimes wondered how different they would be if they had been raised in a white home east of the Mississippi River instead of in a remote, high-country valley where their nearest neighbors were days away and the nearest village with kids their own age usually took a week or more to reach.

Over near the base of the wall something moved. Zach stopped. He had seen what he took to be a large log lying on the lip of the bank but now the log's tail was swishing from side to side. A gator! he realized. He couldn't shoot or the guards would hear. Even if he did, there was no guarantee the shot would strike a vital organ. He'd heard gators were ungodly tough, their thick hides nearly impervious to lead, and wounding it might only incite it into a killing frenzy. Better, Zach thought, to do nothing, and hope the gator decided he wasn't appetizing.

The very next second the odious reptile hissed and slid down the bank into the water as quietly as you please. It swam straight toward him, its eyes and nose and part of its head and back breaking the surface.

Panic gripped Zach, and he almost wheeled and tried to reach the island. But running from a meat-eater usually provoked the animal into attacking, so he stood his ground.

The alligator's tail stopped swishing and it floated the final few yards. Its blunt snout stopped within a foot of Zach's buckskin shirt. Bulging reptilian eyes regarded him with unfathomable interest.

By a supreme effort of raw will, Zach controlled his fear. The old-timers believed predators could smell it, and once that happened, a meat-eater would not stop until its prey was in its belly.

Over nine feet long, the alligator inched nearer. Sawtooth serrations ran the length of its broad back and along its thick tail. Almost as black as the night, it was menace incarnate, a creature nigh invincible in its domain, the armor-plated, toothsome lord of all it surveyed.

For anxious eternities Zach's fate hung in the balance. He braced for a burst of movement and was ready to jam a pistol against its head and squeeze the trigger. He would only have an instant's warning, and he glued his eyes to the tip of its tail, awaiting the telltale flicker that would precede an attack. But unbearably long minutes went by and nothing happened.

Zach could not keep this up indefinitely. His every nerve was stretched taut, his forehead slick with beads of sweat. A drop dripped into his right eye and he blinked to clear it, and just like that the alligator exploded into action. Instinctively Zach backpedaled and lowered his arms. He had already cocked one pistol and now thrust it at the reptile—only the alligator wasn't there. It had whipped around and was swimming rapidly off into the dark depths of the swamp. He stared after it, stupefied by his good fortune, then quickly climbed the bank to the base of the wall, and hunkered.

The gator had disappeared. A bullfrog started up, and somewhere far off a bird shrieked its death cry.

Zach wedged his pistols under his belt and crept forward. He had learned his lesson. It was sheer luck he wasn't dead, and he would not repeat the same mistake.

Not when there was three to four feet of solid soil between the wall and the water.

After only a few strides Zach sat down and stripped off his moccasins. They squished with every step he took, and he couldn't have that. He wrung them out, tugged them back on, wedged both pistols under his belt, and went on, his head tilted to catch sounds, however faint, from above.

As to how to get inside, Zach was at a loss. There wasn't a tree close enough. There were no handholds or footholds. Harold K. Wilkerson was clearly a man who valued his privacy, or else, as the rumors and the hooded figure on the roof hinted, he was a man with vile secrets to hide.

Presently Zach came to the rear of the estate. Over an acre of ground abutted it. This section, too, had been cleared of undergrowth and trees so that no one could approach unseen. A creek split the acre in two halves, flowing out of the swamp.

Zach did not give it much thought until he came to where the creek flowed under the rear wall into the estate. An aqueduct had been built for that express purpose, capped with an iron mesh grate to deter unwanted visitors. Hopping down, Zach stuck his fingers through several small square openings, and pulled.

Much to Zach's amazement, the grating moved. Not much, not more than a quarter of an inch, but it encouraged him to lean his Hawken to one side and grip the grate with both hands. He bunched his shoulders and strained. The metal mesh bit into his fingers, and there was the creak of rusty hinges and the grate moved another quarter of an inch but then would not move at all.

Zach examined it more closely. He had missed spotting a latch at the bottom. Undoing it, he pulled with all his might and the grate slowly creaked open. Holding it with one hand, he grabbed his rifle, ducked into the pitch black, four-foot-wide opening, and lowered the grate behind him.

Furtive slithering gave Zach pause. He was not alone. A tunnel like this, he mused, must be home to many serpents.

Gingerly, bent low at the waist, Zach advanced, moving slowly in case he bumped into a snake. The water was only knee deep but he reckoned that during storms the aqueduct was filled to overflowing.

Something hissed in front of him, and Zach stopped. He could use some light. He had a fire steel, flint, and kindling in his possibles bag but nowhere to place the kindling to light it. All he could do was hope the snake had moved out of his way.

A filmy substance abruptly wrapped itself around Zach's face. He tore at it, not knowing what it was, until it hit him that it must be a spider web. Someone once told him black widows were common in bayou country and that a widow's bite could be excruciatingly painful. "Great," he muttered, but it did not deter him. Gators, cottonmouths, black widows, nothing would keep him from Evelyn, and from exacting his vengeance on the woman who had taken her.

The aqueduct went on forever. Zach swatted dozens of cobwebs and stopped repeatedly when loud hissing warned him his presence was resented. Somehow he made it to the other end without being bitten, only to find another iron grate. Beyond lay woodland so dense starlight failed to penetrate it.

Zach did not see anyone, but he could ill afford a mistake with Evelyn's life in the balance so it was several minutes before he deemed it safe to leave the aqueduct. First, though, he palmed his bowie, sank to his elbows and knees in the water, and tried to wriggle the blade between the grate and the casement to jimmy the latch. It didn't work.

To be foiled by a small metal clasp was frustrating. Putting his shoulder to the grate, Zach tried again. The grate moved but not enough for the knife to slide through. Squatting, he studied the casement. The stone and mortar were of fairly recent workmanship; Annie had told him the estate was less than five years old.

Although it would dull the blade, Zach jabbed at the mortar. When his right arm eventually tired, he switched to the left. Bit by bit, pieces broke off and fell into the water, to be carried away by the sluggish current. In due course he had a gap wide enough to suit him. This time the knife slid through without hindrance, and once that was accomplished, it was the work of moments to undo the clasp.

Zach started to push on the grate, then stopped. Voices reached him, from above, guards patrolling the wall. He worried they had heard him but their voices soon faded. He waited another couple of minutes to be safe, then opened the grate and slipped from the stifling aqueduct out into the welcome embrace of the cool breeze.

Zach was elated. He had done it! He was inside! Now all he had to do was locate Evelyn. His thumb on the Hawken's hammer, he entered the woods. Here was his natural element, not the fetid swamp. Here he was at home. His moccasins made no more than the barest whisper of sound. The shadows were so deep, he was invisible.

A circle of light appeared. It came from a lantern. The glow bathed a wide clearing and a pair of figures in flowing, brown, hooded robes beside a platform of some kind. They were looking at the platform, not toward the woods.

Exercising the stealth of a panther, Zach came to a patch of weeds, and knelt. A pail of water was on the platform and the pair were dipping rags in the pail and wiping the platform down. They worked in spectral silence until one said, "That should do it, don't you think?"

"Mr. Wilkerson could eat off it," said the other.

While one emptied the pail, the second wrung out the rags. "It should be a fine turnout tonight."

"There always is for special occasions like this. Everyone who is anyone will be here."

Their hoods pulled low, the pair headed toward the mansion.

"Mr. Wilkerson is sparing no expense," the man bearing the pail remarked. "All to impress a certain female guest, I hear."

"I didn't think he could call everyone together on such short notice."

"Are you kidding? No one wants to miss a sacrifice. Once the blood starts to flow, the real festivities will begin. I can't wait. The last time, I slept for two days afterward, I was so worn out."

Zach looked at the platform again. Shock coursed through him as he recognized it for what it really was: an altar. Shock compounded by the many dark stains ingrained into the wood. Stains made by one thing and one thing alone: blood.

Human blood.

# Chapter Nine

The Dark Mansion was lit up like the Whiskers and Tails. Light shone in every window and people were scurrying about in a frenzy of preparation. Some wore flowing brown robes. Others were servants. The winding lane from the front gate was lit by lanterns suspended from poles. Carriages were arriving every few minutes and passengers were alighting garbed in peerless finery.

Lying amid aromatic flowers in a garden the light did not reach, Zach King watched carriage after carriage pull up. Merriment was the order of the evening and everyone was laughing and joking among themselves. Some of the carriages left as soon as their passengers climbed out. Others wheeled to a broad clearing and parked to await their owner's convenience.

Twice guards came near his hiding place. Zach was fairly sure they wouldn't spot him; he was more worried about the large dogs straining at the ends of long leashes.

Zach constantly scanned the mansion windows for sign of Evelyn but she did not appear. Several times, though, a woman who might have been Athena Borke moved back and forth past a window on the third floor. It must be the guestroom she was staying in, Zach guessed. Evelyn would either be in the same room or close nearby. Reaching her would take some doing.

Zach caught snippets of the mix of languages spoken; some English, some French, some Spanish. From what he could gather, the guests were keenly anticipating a special event that would take place later. After seeing the blood-stained altar, it did not take a great leap of logic to guess what that event involved.

Another pair of guards came around the corner, a black dog with its nose to the ground in front of them. Zach flattened and saw the dog glance sharply at the flower bed. A hand on one of his pistols, he girded himself to race to the mansion, if need be, and fight his way inside.

The dog angled toward the flowers, forcing the guard holding the other end of the leash to go faster to keep up.

"What in the world has gotten into him?" asked the other guard.

"He probably smells another damn coon or possum. How they keep getting in, I will never know."

"Last night Frank's dog went after a rabbit and chased it for an hour before its leash got tangled. Frank about beat it senseless."

"Come on, boy," urged the man clutching the leash, pulling the dog back. "There's nothing there."

The dog's dark eyes were fixed on the exact spot where Zach was lying. Growling deep in its throat, it clawed at the earth.

"Cut it out, damn you," the guard snapped. "I won't have you running off like Frank's dog did. Behave or else."

"Maybe I should go over there and poke around," his partner suggested.

"Suit yourself. Just don't blame me if you step on a snake. They're all over the place."

His partner stopped short. "Forget it. I hate those damn things. The other day the butler was nearly bit by a big one down in the wine cellar. Scared him so much, he dropped a bottle and broke it. Mr. Wilkerson flew into a rage."

"Poor Arthur."

"Not at the butler, at the copperhead. He took a hoe from the gardener and hacked it to bits."

"That's Mr. Wilkerson for you," the guard with the dog said. "As gentle a soul as ever lived."

Both men laughed and moved on. Zach rose on his elbows. Another carriage was arriving. One of Wilkerson's servants opened the door and lowered the step, and out stepped a ravishing blonde wearing a scintillating diamond necklace and a gown that gleamed as if sewn from spun gold. Zach had never seen anyone so beautiful, and that included his wife.

The radiant vision of loveliness fluttered a fan and laughed merrily as a second woman joined her. Although the second one had lustrous raven hair and was quite demure in her bearing, a definite similarity about the face suggested they were sisters.

A gallant from another carriage approached and the blonde cheerfully offered him her arm. She and her escort had gone a dozen feet when almost as an afterthought, the blonde glanced back and beckoned to the raven-haired one, who dutifully trailed after them.

The mansion was filling not only with guests but with sound—the hubbub of voices and the merrymaking that came from people enjoying themselves to the fullest. Somewhere in there was Evelyn. Pushing up into a crouch, Zach backed from the flower garden, turned, and jogged to the rear of the mansion. He had his choice of several doors and chose one shrouded in shadow. Luck was with him. It wasn't locked, nor did the hinges creak when he eased it open. He had stumbled on a narrow hall, empty at the moment. Slipping inside, he shut the door and hurried to the first room. Books were everywhere, lining sturdy mahogany shelves from ceiling to floor. More books than Zach had ever seen at one time in his whole life.

"A library," Zach said aloud, thinking of his father's prized collection in the cabin in which he had been raised, high in the Rockies. It included the Bible and great works like *The Iliad* and *The Decline and Fall of the Roman Empire*, along with the works of James Fenimore Cooper, one of his father's favorites. Fondly, he recollected how his father had delighted in reading to them when they were younger. Many a cold and icy winter's night, he and Evelyn had lain side by side on the big bearskin rug in front of the crackling fire, their mother sewing quietly in her rocking chair, and listened to their father read for hours on end.

Zach's favorite was *The Iliad*. The stirring battles, the fierce warrior-against-warrior combat thrilled him as no other book could. He felt a kinship to those ancient Greeks, a kinship born of blood, of the counting of coup on an enemy.

Sudden voices down the hall ended Zach's untimely reverie. Whirling, he ran to the doorway. Someone was coming but was not yet in sight. He raced to the back door and slipped outside and stood with his back to it, his heart pounding in his chest. He could not afford to be caught. Harold Wilkerson would demand an explanation and might see fit to have him thrown off the estate, and Zach would be damned if he would go. Not when he was this close.

An urge came over him to cup a hand to his mouth and shout Evelyn's name until she answered but Zach suppressed it and ran to another door that opened onto a short flight of stone stairs leading down. Here it was cool and quiet, and dark. He groped along the wall with

## Join the Western Book Club
## and GET 4 FREE* BOOKS NOW!
### — A $19.96 VALUE! —

## — Yes! I want to subscribe — to the Western Book Club.

Please send me my **4 FREE\* BOOKS**. I have enclosed $2.00 for shipping/handling. Each month I'll receive the four newest Leisure Western selections to preview for 10 days. If I decide to keep them, I will pay the Special Members Only discounted price of just $3.36 each, a total of $13.44, plus $2.00 shipping/handling ($19.50 US in Canada). This is a **SAVINGS OF AT LEAST $6.00** off the bookstore price. There is no minimum number of books I must buy, and I may cancel the program at any time. In any case, the **4 FREE\* BOOKS** are mine to keep.

\*In Canada, add $5.00 shipping/handling per order
for the first shipment. For all future shipments to
Canada, the cost of membership is $16.25 US,
which includes shipping and handling.
(All payments must be made in US dollars.)

**NAME:** _____

**ADDRESS:** _____

**CITY:** _____ **STATE:** _____

**COUNTRY:** _____ **ZIP:** _____

**TELEPHONE:** _____

**E-MAIL:** _____

**SIGNATURE:** _____

an outstretched hand, feeling his way until his fingers made contact with something hanging from a peg.

It was a lantern. One whiff told Zach it was a lard-oil lamp, not kerosene. Groping farther, he discovered a small shelf, and on it, a small box that rattled when he shook it. Moving back to the stairs, where enough light filtered down for him to see what he was holding, he grinned. It was a box of matches, or Lucifers, as some called them, made, according to the label, in Springfield, Massachusetts.

On the frontier, matches were rarely seen. Most frontiersmen still used a fire steel and flint. It wasn't just that matches were expensive, which they were, but that keeping them dry was too much of a headache. Like civilization itself, they were much to fragile to endure the rugged hardships of life in the wild.

Zach had seen them used, though, and now, taking one out, he soon had the lamp lit and was holding it over his head while warily penetrating deeper into the dank underbelly of the mansion. A short stone corridor brought him to a spacious stone chamber lined with rack after rack of wine bottles. Hundreds and hundreds of bottles from all over the world, some with French labels and some with Spanish labels and many more with what Zach took to be Italian labels.

Zach did not know a lot about wine but he did know some vintages were costly. Judging from the vast selection, Wilkerson must have spent more than a small fortune acquiring them.

On the other side of the wine cellar was a door. It opened, but not without noise, and Zach paused to listen before venturing further. He passed several rooms. One was filled with nothing but empty wine bottles. Another contained a work bench and tools. The next interested him most; hanging from long horizontal poles were dozens of flowing brown robes.

Now that Zach thought about it, he had not seen anyone alight from a carriage wearing one, or even carrying one. Yet besides the pair in the clearing, he had seen maybe a dozen others with robes on. Evidently this was where they got them. They afforded Zach an opportunity he couldn't pass up.

Zach tried three on before he found one that suited him. It had to fit loosely enough to conceal the bulge of his pistols and the bowie. His Hawken he reluctantly had to leave behind, hidden in a corner under a pile of food- and wine-stained robes.

Adjusting the hood so that it covered his face, Zach continued down the hall to yet another door. As he was reaching for it, it opened, and a dignified older man in a smart beige jacket and pants bestowed a courteous bow and stood to one side to permit him to pass.

"A good evening to you, sir. The master has sent me for more wine."

Zach took a gamble. "Quite the collection he has, Arthur."

"Indeed. I daresay he treasures his wine almost as much as he treasures nights like this one." Arthur smiled and made for the wine cellar.

How was it, Zach wondered, that everyone could treat the blood-stained altar and all it implied so lightly? Were they as crazy as the "master" of the estate? He had to keep in mind he was dealing with whites and white ways were as strange as strange could be. Yet this, *this*, plumbed new depths of strangeness, depths of which he had never conceived.

Stepping through the doorway, Zach stopped cold as his senses were assaulted by a barrage of colorful sights and loud sounds. He was in an enormous room filled with guests, a room lit by three huge, glittering chandeliers. A room decorated by marvelous works of art in brightly lit nooks; paintings and sculptures the likes of which few people ever saw outside of an art gallery or a museum.

Staying close to the wall, Zach moved into the shadow of an overhang to get his bearings. To his left was the main entrance. On the far right a wide staircase led to the upper floors. To reach them he must wade through a sea of gaily dressed men and women having the time of their lives. Here and there were others in long brown robes. Some had their hoods down, some had them up. Several were women.

Taking a deep breath, Zach moved in among them. No one paid any attention to him until he was halfway there. As he was carefully skirting a particularly loud bunch of half-drunk revelers, a portly man in a gray frock coat snagged his arm and brought him to a stop.

"Here now! Who's this? And why aren't you drinking like the rest of us?" The man had a hooked beak of a nose and puffy lips. Waving a tankard of ale under

Zach's hood, he said, "You need to get into the spirit of things, friend."

Zach sought to pull away but the man was stubborn—and drunk.

"Didn't you hear me? You're supposed to have fun. Here. Let's see who you are." And the man reached for Zach's hood.

Zach was set to slug him and run for the stairs but another man was suddenly there, gripping the portly drunk's wrist.

"Here now, *mon ami*. Is this any way for a gentleman to act?"

The voice was familiar. Zach recognized the Creole whom he had helped against the river rats a few days ago.

"Who asked you to butt in, Fortier?" demanded the stubborn celebrant. "And what are you doing here, anyway? I should think this is hardly to your liking."

"How would you know what I like, Monsieur Bleck?" the Creole stiffly asked. "The reasons for my being here are my own." He twisted Bleck's wrist and Bleck bleated like a stricken sheep and let go of Zach. "That is much better."

"Arrogance ill becomes anyone," Bleck said, mad as a riled hornet.

Fortier bowed civilly to Zach. "You may go about your business, monsieur."

"I thank you," Zach said. "Now we are even." Leaving the puzzled Creole, he soon reached the marble stairs. His first impulse was to take them three at a bound but it would attract unwanted attention. Calmly climbing to the first landing, he paused. Here there were fewer revelers and he could hear himself think.

Several young lovelies in all their finery were giggling and grinning a few yards away. Going over, Zach bowed as he had seen the butler do and adopted a formal tone. "I beg your pardon, ladies, but I was wondering if any of you can tell me where to find Miss Athena Borke?" He had a general idea, but it would be nice to know the exact room.

"Who?" asked the giggliest, whose brown curls bounced at every movement she made, however slight.

"Mr. Wilkerson's special guest," Zach said. "She is staying on the third floor, I believe."

"Never heard of her," said another.

"I have," offered the shortest. "A tall lady with black hair, is she?" When Zach nodded, she said, "I believe they are in the second bedroom on the left off the third-floor landing."

"Thank you." Zach rushed to the next landing and nearly collided with three men in robes coming the other way. All three had their hoods down. Two were young Creoles but the third was a distinguished older gentleman with graying hair and bushy gray sideburns.

It was the older man who inquired, "What is your rush, might I ask?"

Unsure what to say, Zach hesitated until peals of laughter from below hinted at how to respond. "I'm in good spirits, is all."

"Isn't everyone?" the distinguished gentleman said. "But that is never an excuse for poor manners." They descended, the gentleman saying over his shoulder, "I give my guests the run of my home but I expect them to adhere to the amenities."

Zach was startled to realize it was the lord of the manor, Harold K. Wilkerson himself. The man seemed sane enough, but where whites were concerned, looks were often a lie. He impatiently waited until they were far enough down the stairs to not notice what he did next, which was to spin and dash to the second door on the left.

This was it! Zach told himself. He had found his sister at last! He would take her to Kansas and their parents, and within three months they would all be back in their beloved Rockies. Bursting with happiness, he opened the door.

# Chapter Ten

As he opened the door, Zach drew a flintlock from under the folds of his long robe. Evelyn's name was on the tip of his tongue and that's where it stayed. For instead of finding his sister and the vengeful harpy who had abducted her, he found himself staring at two men and two women in formal dress sipping wine. He went to shove the pistol up under his robe but it was too late.

"What the devil is this?" a man with a sweeping mustache demanded. "We came in here for a little privacy."

"Who are you?" asked the other man, "and why in hell are you pointing a gun at us?"

One of the women shot to her feet, her wine glass falling to the plush carpet, and put a hand to her cheek. "My word! He's not white!"

That was when Zach realized his hood had slid back enough to expose most of his face. "I'm sorry," he said, wanting to get out of there before they caused a commotion. "Wrong room." He shut the door and heard one of the men bellow.

"Hold it right there!"

Whirling, Zach slid his right hand up his left sleeve so no one would see the pistol, and made for the landing. He was starting down the stairs when the foursome rushed from the bedroom. The men instantly came after him.

Since running would draw attention, Zach moved briskly but not *too* briskly, nodding at those he passed. He was confident that once he was among the throng of guests filling the great hall, he could elude his pursuers.

Then one of the men cupped his hands to his mouth and shouted down, "Stop that fellow, someone! The one in the robe there!" He went on shouting as he descended.

Several people looked at Zach in puzzlement but no one tried to stop him. He had pulled his hood over his face again, so for all they knew he was one of them. All went well until he was a few steps from the bottom, when a manservant blocked his way.

"Hold it right there, would you, sir? I believe the gentlemen above would like a word with you."

Zach glanced up. The pair were taking the stairs two at a bound. People within earshot were glancing up, wondering what the ruckus was about. "I'm in a hurry. Out of my way," he said, and went to brush by but the servant snatched hold of his robe to stop him, and in so doing, inadvertently pulled his hood down.

A woman gasped.

"There! See!" cried one of those after him. "He's an outsider! Stop him, someone, so we can question him!"

The servant firmed his hold. "Stay right where you are, sir. Something strange is going on here."

Frustration and anger boiled in Zach like molten lava. He had been so close, so very close, and now to have something like this happen! It was enough to make him want to hit someone, and he did, punching the servant on the jaw and knocking him against the rail. A long leap carried him to the floor where he darted toward the distant door to the wine cellar and the room where he had left his Hawken.

"Stop that man! Do you hear me? Stop him and hold him!"

Many did not hear the cry. What with all the talking and laughing and the clink of glasses, only half looked around, and of those, only a dozen or so spotted Zach and joined in the chase.

"Stop him!"

"Someone grab that breed!"

Faces were a blur. Zach was practically running. Caution was no longer advisable, not when at any moment he might be tackled from behind, dashing any hope of being reunited with Evelyn. His plan was to slip out, give things time to calm down, and slip back in.

Ahead the crowd parted. Between Zach and the door stood Harold K. Wilkerson and a bunch of other men in flowing robes. Wilkerson imperiously held a hand aloft, commanding, "Hold it right here."

Zach did no such thing. He veered to go past them, but one of the robed figures sprang to intercept him. He did the only thing he could; he whipped out his pistol and struck the man a glancing blow across the temple. He was not trying to kill, only delay. As the robed figure staggered, a woman screamed. Silence spread across the great hall as everyone turned to see what was happening.

More men leaped to intercept Zach but froze when he trained the flintlock on them and thumbed back the hammer. He only had a dozen feet to go. To clear a path he pointed his gun at those in front of him and they jostled one another in their haste to avoid taking a bullet.

Cries of "Stop him!" and "Get him!" rose from all sides, but Zach made it through the door and slammed it behind him. To discourage them he fired through the panel, shooting high so he would not hit anyone. But someone must have been right outside because there was a loud thump and a piercing shriek.

Zach reached the robe room, shed his robe, and reclaimed the Hawken. As he reemerged a shot cracked and a slug bit into the jamb inches from his head. A torrent of angry men were pouring down the hall after him. He fled, hearing surprised shouts of "It's an Indian!", "A savage!", and "We can't let him get away!"

Zach was seething mad. Everything that could go wrong had gone wrong, and now Athena Borke would hear of the "savage" who was chased from the mansion. Putting two and two together, she would guess who it was and flee, dragging Evelyn along. He had an idea how he could stop her, but to do it, he must reach the front gate before her carriage could.

The inner door to the wine cellar opened and out stepped Arthur, the butler, six or seven dusty bottles balanced in his arms. "I say!" he blurted. "What is the meaning of this, sir?"

Halting, Zach aimed his Hawken at the butler's face. "Out of my way, old man!" No more shots had been fired but those after him were closing the gap.

"Who are you, sir, and how did you get in here, if you do not mind my asking?" Arthur inquired. "Are you aware this is a private party? By invitation only?"

"Don't you see this pistol?" Zach said, wagging it. "Move!"

But the butler stood there as calm as you please, and smiled his polite smile as if they had just met on a street corner and were exchanging pleasantries instead of in a stone-walled corridor with a horde of angry men braying at Zach's heels. "I'm afraid I can't, sir. It appears my employer and some others would like a few words with you."

"Please," Zach said. "I'd rather not shoot you." He was getting too softhearted, he chided himself. He should blow the man's brains out and be done with it.

"That's good to hear, sir, since I would rather not be shot. But it would be remiss of me to permit you to leave. I'm terribly sorry."

Zach's finger tightened on the trigger but he couldn't do it. Let the whites think of him what they would, let the army brand him a renegade and the newspapers describe him as a vicious killer, he would not kill an unarmed man unless he had an exceptionally good reason. As he had when he slit Phineas Borke's throat.

"Damn me," Zach said. Suddenly shoving Arthur aside, Zach bolted into the wine cellar and flung the door shut. He had not noticed there was a bolt, and he threw it just in time. Fists and feet pounded on the other side, shaking the door on its hinges.

"Open up!"

"You can't escape! Give up while you still can!"

Zach ran past the wine racks to the short flight of stairs to the outer world. He was looking back as he raced out into the night and he did not see those who were waiting for him until gun hammers clicked and feral growls warned him things had gone from bad to abysmal.

Four guards were waiting, their guns leveled. Two large black hounds tugged at their leashes, growling and snapping.

"I will only say this once," the tallest guard said. "Drop your weapons and raise your hands in the air or die where you stand."

As quick as Zach was, he could not kill all of them, and the dogs, before the mob broke down the inner cellar door and overtook him. Already he could hear the door splintering. He slowly set the Hawken down, slowly placed his pistols and the bowie beside it.

"Now take two steps to your left and turn your back to us." He was smart, this guard, and stayed far back so Zach could not rush him.

Zach took the two steps and turned.

Out of the mansion spilled all those who were after him. They ringed him, their voices raised in angry accusation. From among them strode Harold K. Wilkerson, and at his sharp gesture, a hostile silence descended.

Wilkerson was not as mad as many of the others; he seemed more curious than anything else. Clasping his hands behind his robe, he walked in a small circle around Zach, intently studying him.

The tall guard came forward. "What do you want us to do with this trespasser, sir?"

A guest had an idea. "We should feed him to the alligators in the swamp. How dare he intrude on our ceremony."

"When he shot through the door he nearly hit George Flanders," said another, "and poor George fainted."

"Let's whip the heathen!" chimed in a third.

Again Wilkerson gestured for quiet. Then, to the tall guard, he said, "Bring him to my study, Mr. Meachum. I very much desire to get to the bottom of this. We can't very well have strangers interfering with our arrangements, now can we?"

Guards and dogs hemmed Zach and he was marched back inside at gunpoint. Both dogs bared their fangs, eager to pounce. Zach had no choice but to allow them to usher him to the room that contained all the books.

Meachum shoved him into a leather chair in front of a polished desk and warned, "Behave yourself or you won't like the consequences."

Several minutes elapsed before the lord of the manor arrived. Wilkerson went straight to a chair behind the desk and sat back, his fingers laced behind his head. "Well now. Where to begin?"

Zach did not say anything.

"You have everyone all in a dither over your antics," Wilkerson said. "Suppose you tell me who you are and why you invaded the privacy of my home?"

"Where's my sister?" Zach demanded.

"I beg your pardon?"

"Evelyn King. She is here with Athena Borke. Don't deny you know her because a carriage brought them here from your hotel earlier today."

Wilkerson glanced at Meachum, who motioned as if to say, "I have no idea what he is talking about." Then Wilkerson said, "Young man, you baffle me. You sneak onto my estate. You violently assault one of my guests and almost shoot another. Now you have the gall to claim I know someone I have never heard of."

"You're lying!" Zach nearly lunged out of his chair. "They're here somewhere and I won't rest until I find them!"

A red tinge crept up Wilkerson's face. "I can't recall the last time anyone had the audacity to call me a liar. I should have you punished for your impertinence."

"Do your worst," Zach spat. "Whip me. Tie me to that altar of yours and torture me. It won't get you anywhere."

"Torture you?" Throwing back his head, Wilkerson laughed uproariously. "Goodness, boy. What sort of monster do you take me for?"

"I've seen the altar," Zach said. "I saw men washing the dried blood off. So don't try to fool me."

"I wouldn't try," said Wilkerson dryly, "since you possess such a marvelous knack for doing that yourself." He leaned on his elbows. "What exactly do you think we do here?"

"You tell me."

Wilkerson thoughtfully regarded him a moment, then rose and moved toward the hall, saying, "Bring him, Mr. Meachum, and no shooting unless he gives you cause."

The other three guards and the dogs accompanied them out the rear of the mansion and across a neatly maintained yard to a barn and several outbuildings nestled amid the trees. At the side of the barn was a corral, and in it, milling about, were more than twenty sheep.

"These," Wilkerson said, "are what we use the altar for, and when we're done, we hold a grand roast and eat them."

"Sheep?" Zach said skeptically. "But the stories people tell about you. The robes you wear."

"I have no control over the gossip of the local cretins. As for the robes, they are part of our revels. Our bacchanals, as we call them, after Bacchus, the Roman god of the vine. Have you heard of him, perhaps, my young savage, or am I wasting my erudition?"

Zach remembered his father reading about the Roman gods, and how they stemmed from the Greek gods, but that was about all he could recollect. "You don't sacrifice people?"

"People?" Wilkerson repeated. This time when he laughed, all the guards joined in. "Are you a lunatic, boy? We eat, we drink, we make merry. That's all there is to it."

"But your robes . . ." Zach said.

"Lend color to our ceremony." Wilkerson looked at Zach as if he did not know quite what to make of him. "I have been accused of many things in my time. It comes with being rich and powerful. But your accusation is surely the stupidest I've ever heard."

Confusion ran rampant through Zach's mind. Every instinct he had told him that Harold K. Wilkerson was telling the truth. "I don't understand," he said softly.

"What to do with you, that's the question. I should have you arrested and thrown behind bars. Or, better yet, into a sanitarium."

From out of the shadows strolled a dashing figure whose sword hilt glittered in the starlight. "Neither will be necessary, monsieur. I humbly ask that you release this adventurous lad into my care."

Wilkerson had to think a moment before he said, "Alain de Fortier, is it not? I have never seen you at any of my functions before."

"I had a special reason for coming tonight," the jaunty Creole answered. "But, alas, I cannot find her."

"Ah, yes. Your fondness for the ladies is legendary." Wilkerson smiled, but thinly. "As for my unwanted visitor, what is he to you that you should intercede on his behalf?"

"He once interceded on my behalf and saved my life. And a gentleman always pays his debts."

Wilkerson pondered, then said, "Very well. I will check, and if none of my guests cares to press charges, neither will I. But I advise you to vacate him from these premises as soon as I give my consent."

"As you wish, Monsieur Wilkerson."

Zach was trying to make sense of everything that had happened and to reconcile it with the information the hotel driver had given him. "I thank you," he said to de Fortier, "but I can manage on my own."

The Creole indicated the rifles still trained on him. "So I see."

# Chapter Eleven

The carriage came to a stop. Zach climbed out and peered the length of a narrow street overlooked by balconies with wrought-iron railings. "What part of the city is this again?"

Alain de Fortier was paying their fare. "We call it *Vieux Carre*, or the French Quarter, as it is more commonly known." He adjusted his sword and headed down the equally narrow sidewalk. "We call these *banquettes*," he said, stomping the sidewalk with one of his costly leather boots.

"And this is where we'll find him?" Zach asked. They had been to The Harvest House, where Alain had quizzed the desk clerk about the various drivers, trying to establish which one Zach had talked to. The clerk was reluctant to cooperate until Alain deposited several gold coins in his palm.

"I can't let you do that," Zach had protested. "It's your money."

"Which I would not be alive to spend if you had not saved me from those footpads," said Alain, demonstrating infallible Creole logic. "So we will hear no more about it, *s'il vous plaît.*"

It was pushing midnight and the district was deserted except for a few individuals hurrying home from taverns or more earthy pleasures. To Zach the narrow streets were a maze. In the dark he could not pick out landmarks as he would in the wilds and after a few turns his sense of direction was askew. A quick glance at the North Star reassured him.

Alain had one hand on his sword hilt at all times, as seemed to be his habit. He was also never at a loss for words. "A most sad tale you have shared, *mon ami.* You have my utmost sympathies. And I vow on my honor as a gentleman and a de Fortier that I will not rest until your precious sister is found."

Zach was not comfortable relying on another; from his earliest childhood he had been a loner, and that was how he liked it. "There's no need for you to get involved."

"Would you refuse me my debt of honor?" Alain asked a trifle indignantly. "We have been all through this several times now. I should think you would do me the courtesy of not bringing it up ever again."

"Let's talk about you then," Zach said. "What were you doing at Wilkerson's mansion? Their bacchanals are not to your liking, I gather?"

"*Non*, they are not. My blood runs as hot as the next man's, but getting drunk on wine and running about in the dark chasing giggling women is not my idea of making love. A man must have his dignity."

"I would say you have plenty." Zach was growing fond of this talkative rake, despite himself.

"*Vous êtes bien aimable.* You are too kind."

"Then why were you there?"

Alain did not answer right away. "Very well. I suppose it is only fair since you have been so frank with me." His sigh filled the street. "I was there because of a woman, I regret to admit."

"What is there to regret?" Zach wondered. A cat came out of the shadows, arched its back and hissed at them, and darted off. "I had the notion you're fond of them."

"More than you can possibly imagine," Alain confessed. "But that's just it. I have always pursued the ladies with great enthusiasm. And I have—how shall I put this?—dallied with more than most ten men do in a lifetime."

"I've only ever pursued one," Zach said. "But I'm not so sure she didn't lay a snare for me to walk into."

"Therein lies my problem," was Alain's forlorn comment.

"You've been smitten?"

"*Oui*, monsieur. I can not stop thinking about this one woman. *Une femme! Moi!* Who has bedded dozens! I see her in every window; I smell her in every flower. It drives me insane, this image of her. Yet I am drawn to her as a moth to the flame."

Zach noticed a woman watching them from a balcony. "Some folks call that love. I hear it's perfectly normal."

"For others, perhaps, but not for Alain de Fortier! Love is for lesser mortals, not me. It is unthinkable that I should succumb."

Damned if he wasn't serious, Zach thought, and fought down a grin. "Does this gal have a name?"

"*Oui*. Rachelle Chantel Prunella Cuvier." Alain said the words like each was a priceless pearl. "She is petite and dark and quiet and shy, all the traits I have always liked least in women. Yet she is the one whose eyes and lips are seared in my mind. I ask you, have you ever heard anything so silly?"

"You are keeping track of where we're going?" Zach thought to mention.

"I was born here, raised here. I know this district like I do the cut of my clothes. Never fear. I will bring you right to his doorstep." Alain came to a corner and turned left. "What am I to do, my young friend? Do I sail off to Paris for six months and hope I can drink Rachelle out of my system? Or do I tell her how I feel and risk the consequences?"

"Ever think she might feel the same about you?"

"Which is precisely the consequence I fear most. For if she does, what then? Honor demands I get down on bended knee and ask for her hand, but I am not ready to tie myself to one woman, not when the world is full of charming conquests to be made."

"There's no explaining love," Zach said. Had someone told him ten years ago that he would one day marry a white woman, he would have laughed in his face. Life had a habit of springing the unexpected.

"But is it love? Or infatuation?" Alain shook his head. "Rachelle is so different, so unlike all the others, that maybe it is the difference I adore and not her, yes?"

"You're talking in circles," was Zach's opinion.

"Maybe so, maybe so. But now you can see the other reason I enjoy helping you. For a while it will take my mind off Rachelle and permit me to think with a clear head." Alain touched his chest. "If only it would do the same for my heart." He abruptly stopped at a small white wooden gate. "This is the place."

It opened onto a patio rimmed by banana trees. Alain strode to a door and knocked loud enough to wake up everyone for a block around. A light came on and someone hollered, "Who's there? Do you know how late it is?"

"We must talk with you, monsieur, on an urgent matter of life and death," Alain announced. "Admit us this instant or we will kick your door down."

"Like hell I will!" was the irate reply. "I don't know who you are. Go away or I will send for the law."

Alain winked at Zach. "Is that what you would have us tell your employer? Very well. But do not blame us if it costs you your job."

"Mr. Wilkerson?" By now the man was at the door. "What does he have to do with this?"

"He is the one who sent us," Alain lied. "How else do you think we obtained your address, Monsieur Hobart? Now will you open up and answer our questions or must we come back tomorrow with Monsieur Wilkerson?"

A bolt rasped and locks were turned and Hobart warily cracked the door a few inches. He was in a nightshirt, his hair rumpled, and holding a lamp over his head. "What sort of questions?"

Alain turned to Zach. "Is this him?" At Zach's nod, Alain smiled and turned back to Hobart and drew his sword. "Now then," he said, pressing the tip against the driver's abdomen, "you will be so kind as to explain why you deceived my friend today?"

"Your friend!" Hobart sputtered, scared but not yet scared enough. He held the lamp higher, and gasped. "You!"

"Me," Zach said. He would have liked to drag him outside and beat him to a senseless pulp but it would not gain them the information they so dearly needed.

"I am waiting, monsieur," Alain said. "And I am not always the most patient of men."

Hobart swallowed, then claimed, "I have no idea what you're talking about. Go away, I tell you!"

Alain's wrist flicked and a small nick appeared on the side of Hobart's neck. It was not deep but it drew blood. "Consider that friendly encouragement. I suggest your memory improve, monsieur, or I will begin cutting off

113

body parts. Take your left ear, for instance." The sword's tip rose to Hobart's earlobe. "You can get by without it, but ears have some value, do they not?"

"You're crazy!"

The sword moved ever-so-slightly and a small cut appeared. "Speak to us," Alain demanded. "Why did you lie to my friend and send him on a wild goose chase?"

Hobart licked his thick lips. His Adam's apple bobbed. He gazed past them, up and down the street, then at the nearby buildings. In a whisper he said, "She promised to have me killed if I breathed a word to anyone."

Zach stepped forward. "She? Athena Borke?"

Nodding, Hobart said thickly, "She told me she was playing a joke and asked me to play along. That when I returned to the hotel and you approached me about her, I was to say I had taken you to Mr. Wilkerson's estate. Then she gave me twenty dollars." He spread his hands. "That's all there was to it."

A troubling sense of unease filled Zach. "How did she know I would talk to you?" It implied she had known he was in New Orleans the whole time; had known, in fact, that he had seen her leave the hotel with Evelyn. But that was impossible, he assured himself. Or was it? Had she spotted him down the street?

"You would have to ask her," Hobart said. "All I can tell you is that she was quite pleased with herself. Not the little girl, though. The girl looked sad."

A knife seared Zach's insides. "Did the girl say anything? Anything at all?"

"Only once that I heard. The woman had said something about leading you around by the nose and laughed, and the girl got so mad, I thought she would tear into her. But all the girl did was say that one day the woman would get her just desserts, whatever that means." Hobart paused. "Is this about the pony you were planning to sell them?"

Zach had forgotten his lie. "That little girl is my sister and that woman has kidnapped her."

Hobart glanced from Zach to Alain and back again. "You're serious?"

The Creole's sword moved to within a whisker's-width of the driver's left eye. "Never more so. This Borke woman used you. She hoped that my friend would go to Monseiur Wilkerson's and have a not so pleasant encounter with his guards and their dogs. *Comprenez-vous?*"

"My word," Hobart said. "I had no idea. Honest to God I didn't."

"Be that as it may, you nearly got my friend killed," Alain said. "Now you will make amends by telling us where you really took Mademoiselle Borke and her young charge. And I warn you: Lying to me will bring swift and terrible retribution."

"Sure, sure, I'll tell you whatever you want," Hobart bleated. "Just don't stick me with that thing."

"We are waiting," Alain said.

"I took them to The Regal Club."

"Eh?" Alain took a step back. "What would Mademoiselle Borke possibly want there?"

"How would I know?" Hobart said. "I dropped them off and she paid me half a year's wages to keep quiet about it. Then they went inside and that was the last I saw of them."

"She took the little girl in?"

Zach did not understand why the Creole was so shocked. It heightened his anxiety for his sister's welfare.

"She didn't have much say in the matter," Hobart was relating. "The Borke woman had hold of her wrist and practically dragged her."

"And you didn't protest? A girl, taken *there*?" Alain looked fit to thrust his sword through the driver's torso.

Hobart paled. "Hey, I was only doing my job. I take people to all kinds of places, places I wouldn't set foot in for love nor money. But I can't control what others do."

"*Mon Dieu!*" Alain exclaimed, and lowered his weapon. "All right. You may go back to your rest. But remember my warning. If you have lied, the next time you see me will be the last time you ever see anyone."

Hobart was quick to slam the door and throw the bolt, and then to find his courage and shout, "If you ever set foot here again, I'll shoot you on sight!"

Alain moved toward the street, his head bowed, muttering under his breath in French.

"What is it?" Zach asked, catching up. "Why are you so upset?"

"It is your sister, *mon ami*. Or to be more specific, the establishment where Mademoiselle Borke has taken her."

"The Regal Club? What about it?" To Zach the name sounded respectable enough. "Have you been there?"

"Only once, and I vowed never to set foot over the threshold ever again." Alain turned left at the gate. "There is no worse den of evil in all of New Orelans. The despicable vermin who owns it, Martin Vasklin, likes to put on airs and act the gentleman, but no one in the city is more despised."

The name jarred Zach's memory. "Vasklin, you say? I've run into him." He related the incident at the Whiskers and Tails, and described the greasy man with the greasy hair.

"That is him, all right," Alain confirmed. "Just to look at him makes one's skin crawl."

"What about this club of his? What goes on there?"

"You do not want to know," Alain said. "It caters to the worst in human nature, to depraved desires and unspeakable longings. The front room is a gambling den where every card is marked and every wheel rigged. In the back rooms . . ." Alain could not bring himself to finish.

Zach gripped the Creole by the shoulders. "Be truthful with me. I must know. Why would Athena Borke take my sister there? What would they do with a girl Evelyn's age?"

Alain de Fortier grimaced. "Their depravity has no limits, I am afraid. There is nothing they would not do. Nothing at all."

"You don't mean . . . ?"

"Yes, my friend. I am afraid I most certainly do."

# Chapter Twelve

The Regal Club did not live up to its name. It was situated near the waterfront, in a part of New Orleans Alain de Fortier described as "a haunt of killers and thieves, a place no decent person would be caught dead at any hour of the night or the day."

Zach's fear for Evelyn had become a gnawing ache inside him. He could think of nothing but her, of what she might be going through. Grimly, he silently repeated his solemn promise to himself that the moment he came within reach of Athena Borke, she was dead.

The building that housed The Regal Club was like all the others on the block; squat and ugly, its walls speckled with grime, its windows dark pits covered by dirty curtains.

On the stoop lounged three toughs playing dice. One sneered and said, "What have we here? A half-breed? He's not getting through the door."

"Pardon, monsieur," Alain said. "But he is with me and where I go, he goes. So would you care to step aside or be run through? The choice is yours."

The tough had a knife but before he could pull it one of the others said, "Hold on. Mr. Vasklin wouldn't like it. He knows this Creole."

Dripping disdain, Alain marched past them. Zach started to follow but an arm was thrust in front of him.

"Guns aren't permitted, breed. Your friend is well aware of that. Blades, yes. Firearms, no."

Zach glanced at Alain, who scowled and nodded.

"We'll watch over them," the scalawag said. "Nothing will happen to them, and they are yours to take when you leave."

"You can believe him," Alain said. "It's money they steal, not guns."

Although loathe to part with them, Zach handed his rifle and pistols over. He kept the bowie. His back itched as he entered after Alain. The reek of liquor and other, less savory odors, was like a physical punch to the gut. On the wall was a sign: MEMBERS ONLY.

"Pay it no heed," Alain said. "Vasklin put it up because it makes him think he is someone special when he is not. He has long entertained pretensions of being a gentleman but all he will ever be is a blackguard."

The place was a cave. Only a few lamps were lit, and those strategically placed as to render most of the tables and the bar half in shadow. Zach felt as if he had just entered a den of grizzlies. Or perhaps wolves would be more appropriate. Many of the stares cast his way were filled with the familiar taint of bigotry. He held his head high and met each coldly.

It was one o'clock in the morning but the club was packed. Every foot of floor space was crammed, the bar was four deep. Games of chance were underway. Some players were bucking the tiger. Others were engrossed in poker. Clouds of cigar smoke wreathed the ceiling, stray tendrils twisting and curling as if they were alive.

Despite all the people, the place was uncommonly quiet. These were not the festive, carefree patrons from Kitty's. These were hard men and hard women whose capacity for laughter had long since died. These were predators to whom life was a continual struggle for survival, and to whom a game of chance might mean the difference between their next meal and going hungry. They trusted no one, they cared for few.

Alain's expression was as somber as those around him, yet he stood out from them as the sun stood out from the moon. His expensive clothes, his air of sophistication, were as out of place as a bowl of fine china on a table of crude clay crockery.

A painted woman came up to him, her lips as red as strawberries, her dress as tight as skin. Clinging to his shoulder, she whispered in Alain's ear. Alain shook his head and sought to move on but she pulled at his jacket, and suddenly he had her by the throat and was twisting her left wrist to force her to release the poke she had slipped from his pocket. He did not say anything. Neither did she. When she let go, he pushed her, and she sniffed as if insulted and flounced off in search of an easier victim.

"How did you know?" Zach asked. "Did you feel her take it?"

"I did not have to," Alain said. "As much as it shames me to admit it, I am as much at home in a den of iniquity like this as I would be in the most elegant parlor. Much of my life has been grossly misspent, my friend."

Zach was searching for Athena Borke. It was too much to expect her to be there after so many hours had gone by, unless she was in one of the back rooms. He saw a door at the rear and was about to make for it when out from among the wolves stepped a weasel.

Martin Vasklin's swarthy features were a mirror of all that was corrupt and vicious in human beings. His greased hair, his slick mustache, his tailored clothes could not disguise his vile nature. "Well, well, well. As I live and breathe. If it isn't Alain de Fortier."

"Monsieur Vasklin," the Creole said.

"Correct me if I'm wrong, but didn't you say you would never set foot in my club again?" Vasklin taunted. "That it was beneath your dignity to—how did you put it?" Vasklin snapped his fingers. "Ah, yes. It was beneath your dignity to associate with riffraff."

"I am here on my friend's behalf," Alain said. "Otherwise I would not have graced your doorstep."

"Is this business or pleasure?"

"It is of great personal importance," said Alain.

"Oh really?" Vasklin raked Zach from head to toe with a look of poorly concealed contempt. "Part Indian, is he not? And you really must tell me who his tailor is. Only country bumpkins come into the city in buckskins these days." Vasklin's forehead knit. "Wait a minute. I know him from somewhere. But where?"

Zach hoped Vasklin had not had a good look at his face at Whiskers and Tails. It had all happened so fast, and he had been wearing the white jacket and pants of the kitchen staff, that maybe Vasklin wouldn't remember. But he should have known better. No one ever forgot someone who slugged them on the jaw.

"I remember now! You're the bastard who hit me! The lout who interrupted our card game, and Kitty had thrown out."

"You hit him?" Alain said.

"He wouldn't keep his hands to himself," Zach explained.

Martin Vasklin's slick mustache was twitching. "You are a fool to come here. No one lays a hand on me and lives to brag of it."

Alain stepped between them. "Strike him and you must deal with me. He is under my protection."

Zach was well able to take care of himself and was set to say so but the Creole's comment dampened some of Vasklin's anger.

"Very well. I can demand satisfaction later. But make no mistake. I will have it, one way or the other, as is my right as a gentleman."

"We would like to talk in private," Alain said. "Is there any chance we can go to your office?"

"Why not?" Vasklin snapped his fingers and two underlings fell into step in front and in back of them. "Follow me."

Alain leaned toward Zach to whisper, "Be careful, *mon ami*. Our host does not have a forgiving bone in his body. He will strike at you when you least expect, so above all, do not turn your back to him."

"I won't," Zach said. "But what about Evelyn? Shouldn't we search the back rooms before we do anything else?"

"Bear with me a few minutes," Alain said quietly. "I know this scoundrel better than you. If we demand the right to search the premises, he will refuse. We must trick him into thinking it is his idea."

Zach decided to let the Creole handle things, provided it did not take too long. He could not stand the idea that Evelyn might be so close he could practically reach out and touch her.

Vasklin ushered them down a murky hall and into a room with a cluttered desk and several cheap chairs. Opening an oaken cabinet, he took out a bottle of whiskey and three glasses and set them on the desk. Only after he had filled them halfway and given one to each of them did he sink into the chair, take a long sip, and sigh. "Now then, Fortier. Tell me more about the reason for your visit."

"As I told you," Alain said, with a nod at Zach, "it is

on his behalf. This is his first visit to our fair city and he would like to enjoy our varied entertainments."

"So take him to the theater or to Le Grande," Vasklin suggested. "I hear that is where you spend most of your time these days."

"They do not offer quite the same type of entertainment you do. You know the kind I mean." Alain grinned and winked.

Vasklin pretended not to understand. "No, I don't. Why don't you spell it out for me?"

Zach could see he was doing it on purpose to make de Fortier uncomfortable.

"I can speak for myself," he interjected, but Alain held up a hand.

"No, that is quite all right, *mon ami*. If Monsieur Vasklin takes perverse delight in having me talk about such things, then, as his guests, we will oblige him." Alain's eyes glittered like twin pieces of quartz. "My friend here is, as you rightly observed, part Indian. His people have tastes more in keeping with your own than with mine."

It was a bald-faced lie but Vasklin was too ignorant to realize it, and inwardly Zach chuckled.

"Be more specific." Zach could tell that Vasklin took pleasure from making Alain give the details.

"Everyone knows that certain carnal delights can only be found under your roof. No one else dares offer them. In that respect you are truly in a class by yourself."

"True. And do you know why that is? It is not because I am a shrewder businessman, although I am undeniably shrewd. It is not because I am less afraid of the law, although, yes, my courage has never been questioned. No, it is because I am the only person in New Orleans who scoffs at the morals of the masses. The only person who is not afraid of God."

"Now it is you who must be more specific," Alain said.

Vasklin was enjoying himself. "Let us take Kitty as an example. Her house of delights is famed throughout the city and the state. She offers girls in all shapes and sizes. But none younger than sixteen. And why? Because there is a moral line she will not cross. But not me. I cross any moral line because I have no morals. And do you know why I don't?"

Neither Zach nor Alain responded.

"I have no morals because I do not believe there is a God who enforces some silly moral code by which we all must live. Life is what it is and we are who we are and that is all there is to it."

"I refuse to accept that," Alain said.

"Naturally. You are as misguided as everyone else. But once you look at the world through my eyes, once you see God for the fiction He is, a whole new world opens up to you. A world where you can do whatever you please. Where there is no right or wrong but only what is best for you at any given moment."

"I must confess, Martin, that you ponder things more deeply than I ever gave you credit for," Alain said. "But the fact remains I could not disagree more."

Vasklin shrugged. "No one expects you to agree, least

of all me." He shifted his attention to Zach. "Now then. Exactly what kind of entertainment do you seek, half-breed?

Alain answered instead. "Young girls are his fancy."

"Really? I had no idea Indians went in for that sort of thing. You learn something new every day." Vasklin paused. "But you have come to the right place. I have the youngest under my roof you will find anywhere."

Zach wondered if it was as hard for Alain to mask his loathing as it was for him. He would dearly love to draw his bowie and turn Martin Vasklin's neck into a fountain. "May I see them? I would like to pick the one I want."

"Of course, of course. The customer always gets to choose," Vasklin said, and rose. "Come with me and I will show off my little princesses." He polished off his whiskey and smacked the glass down on the desk.

His heart hammering, Zach followed Vasklin down the hall to a room on the left. The only item of furniture was a bed, and seated at one end, combing her hair, was a girl dressed much as the women out in the club.

"This is Ardeth," Vasklin said. "For a hundred dollars you can spend an hour with her doing whatever you like."

"She does not interest me," Zach said, unable to look her in the eyes.

"Her hair is too light? Is that it? You must prefer girls with hair the color of your own. Come then. I have just the one."

127

A different room, a different bed, a different girl, no more than a child, but this time with long black hair, her eyes twenty years older than they should be.

"This is Daphne," Vasklin introduced her. "She is as experienced as they come. She costs fifty dollars more an hour but it is money wisely spent." He laughed lecherously. "What do you say?"

Zach turned away. "She does not suit me, either."

A third room, a third girl, a girl who looked enough like Evelyn to cause Zach's throat to constrict and his temperature to rise. "Enough of this," he said. There was only so much he could stand.

"What is wrong?" Vasklin asked, genuinely puzzled.

"I am looking for my sister," Zach revealed, "and I have reason to believe she is here."

"Oh really?" Vasklin glanced at the four men who had followed them and the quartet produced pistols from under their clothes.

Zach might have leaped at him if not for Alain de Fortier, who seized his arm and whispered in his ear, "*Non! Non!* Now is not the time."

Vasklin had his hands on his hips. "So it's not entertainment you desire, after all. I treated you cordially and you deceived me. Very well." He pointed toward the club. "My men will escort you off the premises. Never set foot in here again if you know what is good for you." Vasklin turned to Alain. "The only reason I don't kill the two of you where you stand is because you have many friends in high places who might take it into their heads to come after me, and I never court trouble when it can be avoided."

Zach was a volcano on the verge of erupting. Somehow he controlled himself until they were outside and he had been given his guns, but the moment he had them, he whirled to charge back in.

"Be sensible," Alain cautioned, pushing him toward the corner of the block. "You would not get past the first table."

"Evelyn might be in there!" Zach fumed.

"I know, I know. But this is more than the two of us can handle. What we need are allies, and I know exactly where to find them."

# Chapter Thirteen

It was close to two in the morning when they arrived at Whiskers and Tails, which pulsed with light and sound. At a question from Zach, Alain de Fortier replied, "No, the city never sleeps. Many are night creatures who rarely set foot outdoors until after the sun has gone down. I know, because I am one of them."

James and his father were at their posts, their uniforms starched and immaculate. The father smiled at the Creole and said warmly, "Mr. de Fortier, what a pleasure to see you again." His smile faded. "But the gentleman with you, I am sorry to say, can't be admitted. It would cost us our jobs."

"Fetch your mistress, Franklyn," Alain requested. "She and I must have words."

Fifteen minutes later, out sashayed Kitty, as dazzling as a rainbow. Her manner was reserved. "While I am pleased to see you again, Alain, I am not so pleased by the company you keep. He sows chaos like a hurricane. To say nothing of the dog he killed."

"Dog?" Alain said, and glanced at Zach in reproach. "You said nothing about any dog." Then, smiling, he placed a hand on Miss Kitty's arm. "But since when have you held grudges, lovely one? My friend regrets it, I am sure, and once you hear his sad tale, perhaps you will think more favorably of him." He recited all that Zach had told him about Evelyn's abduction, ending with, "And there you have it, mademoiselle. Are you still upset with him?

"I won't excuse the dog, if that's what you're thinking," Kitty said. "But I don't hold his behavior against him, either. I rescind my order. Your friend may come in. But be advised: If this is a ruse, I will banish the both of you for life."

"*Ma cherie,*" Alain said, bowing and kissing her hand. "You wound me to the quick. I would as soon lose an arm or leg as risk losing your friendship. Haven't I ever mentioned how your beauty has inspired many a dream I dare not repeat?"

"Flatterer," Kitty said, but she was enormously pleased. "I swear, that velvet tongue of yours could talk a woman into all kinds of mischief. No wonder ladies of virtue live in fear of you."

"*Moi?*" Alain said, playing his part to perfection. "Where did you ever hear such a thing? I would never prevail on a lady to do anything she did not already want to do."

"You are too dashing by half," Kitty said, and hooking her arm through his, led them inside.

Zach did not know what the Creole had in mind. So he was considerably surprised when Kitty conducted them to the same room as the other night, to the same table where another poker game was in progress. Only this time Captain Massey and Martin Vasklin were not taking part. Another man he recognized was, though; Duncan, the professional gambler in the black frock coat, who was almost as handsome in his way as de Fortier. It was beside the gambler's chair that they stopped.

"My abject apologies, Duncan," Kitty said. "I regret interrupting your game but I have a guest here who insists he must speak to you about an affair of the utmost importance."

Duncan pushed chips to the center of the table and turned, an eyebrow arching quizzically. "I play cards all night, every night, without fail. It is my livelihood. You know that, Alain."

"*Oui*," Alain said. "But there is a girl being held against her will in a den of vipers who needs rescuing and I thought you might be interested."

"Your misadventures, Alain, are your own. Why involve me in another of your many conquests?" Duncan turned back to the table as if the matter were settled.

"When I said 'girl,' I meant 'girl,'" Alain clarified, and nodded at Zach. "It is his younger sister. She has been kidnapped. And when I tell you into whose clutches she has fallen, you will be more than interested, I promise."

"Your friend has my sympathy," Duncan said, "but New Orleans has people who are paid to keep the peace."

"But we both know they are new and untested and have a tendency to look the other way when a few coins are dropped into their palms. It's better in this instance to handle this personally and perhaps rid the city of a cancer in the bargain."

"Quit talking in riddles. Who is this cancer you speak of?"

"Martin Vasklin."

A remarkable thing happened. Duncan sat as still as a statue, then turned his cards over, announced to the other players, "I regretfully fold and bid you goodnight." Sliding back his chair, he rose. Among the cards he had turned over were three aces. "Tell me everything."

They settled into plush chairs in a corner of the room and over steaming cups of coffee Zach related his quest and the reason for it. When he was done the gambler took a few sips before commenting.

"I can hardly blame Miss Borke for wanting you dead after what you did to her brothers. But I can fault her lack of judgment in involving your sister, who is an innocent in all this." Duncan set down his cup and looked at Alain. "Vasklin and I have been bitter enemies for years, even before I killed his brother in a duel. He would dearly love to repay me. For my part, I would love to have him join his brother in hell. And now you have given me the perfect excuse."

"I thought I could count on you," Alain said.

"There are conditions, however. We do this my way or I do not take part. The friends I will call on might lose their lives, so it is not to be undertaken lightly."

"Friends?" Zach asked.

"Be patient, *mon ami*," Alain urged. "All will be made clear soon enough."

Duncan took them down the hall to another room and another card game in progress. At the table sat an older man in an identical frock coat with a large stack of chips in front of him. "Fontaine, I have need of you."

Fontaine's gray eyes darted to Zach. "Oh? Does it involve money, women, or lead? Or preferably all three?"

"It involves Martin Vasklin."

In the act of reaching for a card, Fontaine grinned a grin as cold is ice. "You don't say? It's about time that miserable blackguard received what is coming to him." He excused himself from the game. "Is anyone else joining our little party or is this an indulgence in suicide?"

"Follow me," Duncan said.

Downstairs was a lounge in which men and women freely mixed, freely drank, and freely fondled. On a settee under a painting of plump women reclining naked on a bed of roses sat another man in a frock coat with a plump woman of his own on his lap. Short of build, no more than five feet in height, he nonetheless had broad shoulders and arms worthy of a wrestler. At the moment he was nibbling a path from the plump woman's cleavage to her neck while she giggled and squirmed in delight.

"Thorne," Duncan addressed him.

"Go away. Can't you see I'm giving this young lady the treat of her life?"

"It's Vasklin."

Thorne stopped nibbling and straightened, much to the woman's obvious disappointment. "Can it be? I have been urging you to do this for months. You have let that cur live too long."

"An oversight I will soon remedy," Duncan pledged. "But think carefully. There will be more of them than there will be of us, and desperate men sell their lives dearly."

"So the odds are not in our favor? So what? Our whole lives are dedicated to bucking the odds, are they not?" Thorne pecked the woman's cheek, lowered her to the settee, and stretched. "I know Fontaine well but these other two are new to me. Perhaps you would introduce them."

The formalities took five minutes, and when Duncan was done, Thorne patted both his sleeves and said, "I am as ready as I will ever be. But tell me, how many more of us will there be?"

"Four should do it."

The first was down the street in a tavern that catered to the higher class of the city's social strata. At a plush booth sat a cadaverous man with a pale complexion and white hair that contrasted sharply with his black frock coat. He was rolling dice, his chin propped in the other hand, as bored as bored could be. At sight of them he brightened. "Duncan! Thorne! And Fontaine, too! Please tell me you have a high-stakes game in which you wish me to take part."

"No such luck, Quinton," Duncan said. "We're on our way to slay a dragon and I thought you might like to throw in with us."

"Will a lot of blood be spilled?"

"I should think so, yes."

"Then I'm your man. Anything for some excitement." Quinton jumped up and had to duck his head to avoid a low beam. He was ungodly tall. Six feet eight or nine, Zach guessed. "And I still owe you for covering my back during that disagreement a few weeks ago." He did not ask who they were going up against. He did not seem to care.

Their next stop was an elegant gambling house notable for its lack of women. Only men were present, conducting games of chance in quiet dignity. Duncan steered them to where two men in matching brown jackets and vests were playing, of all things, chess. "Richard. Owen. Might I impose on you a moment?"

Richard pulled a white handkerchief from his left sleeve, raised it to his nose, and sniffed. "You can impose on me any time."

"Ignore him," Owen said, moving one of his bishops. "He has been in a mood all day. You would think he was female, how he carries on sometimes." Owen crossed his legs and folded his arms. "What can we do for you?"

"I seem to recall one of you nearly came to blows with Martin Vasklin a month or so ago," Duncan mentioned.

"That pig!" This from Richard, who throttled his handkerchief as if it were Vasklin's neck. "You should have heard what he called me. Right in front of everyone. I would have killed him on the spot but Owen insisted I behave. He spoils all my fun."

"Would you like a chance to repay Vasklin for his insult?" Duncan asked.

Richard came out of his chair. "Yes!"

"No," Owen said.

Richard frowned and leaned on the table. "Are you my mother now? Give me one good reason why not?"

"We might be killed."

"I said a good reason. You always let emotion cloud your judgment. Typical epicene. Well, I say Duncan is our friend and we would be remiss not to help him." Richard took a cloak from a hook on the wall and swirled it about his slim shoulders. "Are you coming or will you sit there pouting the rest of the night?"

"You can be insufferable," Owen said, but he stood. "Just remember this the next time you go off on one of your tirades about how I am more of an anchor than a sail."

"Tirades, are they?" Richard countered heatedly. "Why, I have half a mind to end our friendship here and now, you unappreciative tart."

"Tart?" Zach said to Alain.

"I'll enlighten you later."

Duncan intervened by saying, "Gentlemen, gentlemen, if you please. Save your bickering. We only have until daylight and there is much yet to do."

Their next stop was on the waterfront, a gin joint that was a trial for any nose, with peeling walls and a floor that had not been swept in a month of Saturdays. At a small table sat a member of the gambling fraternity in a well-worn black frock coat. His sandy hair was unkempt, his chin speckled with bristles, and his blue eyes had a watery quality about them. A thin cigar dangled from his lips. He acknowledged Duncan with a nod. "Out recruiting, are we?"

"One more would go a long way to bettering the odds," was Duncan's reply. "I was hoping you would throw in with us, Vin."

"On whom are we waging war?" Vin inquired while shuffling.

"Who is the one man you hate most in the world? The one you blame for your sister's disappearance but against whom you could never find proof?"

Fire leapt into Vin's watery eyes. "Martin Vasklin? Am I dreaming or is this real?"

"All too real," Duncan said. "May I count you in?"

"Need you ask?" Scattering the cards, Vin stood. He swayed, gripped the edge of the table, and smiled. "I would not miss this for the world. I thank you for thinking of me. It means a lot."

"Are you sure you are up to this?" Duncan asked.

"I will crawl if I have to, and rip out his throat with my teeth. Just do not deny me this chance." Propped against the wall was a black cane which Vin retrieved and twirled, growing more steady with each step. "See? It is amazing what we can do when we put our minds to it."

Through the dark city they filed, down one dark and dusky street after another, taking a circuitous route, Duncan informed Zach, so their quarry would not be alerted to their coming. With their black frock coats and black hats, the gamblers lent a funereal air to the procession.

Zach found himself walking beside Vin, who was humming. "You're awful happy for someone who might be dead by sunrise."

"All of us might," Vin said. "But well I should be. A year and a half ago my younger sister vanished without a trace. There was talk, rumors only, that Vasklin was involved. My sister, you see, was quite lovely. Exceptionally so. But although I frequented his club for months and did all in my power to find her, I never did."

"I am sorry," Zach said.

"No false sympathy, if you please. Life is cruel enough without that."

"It isn't false. My own sister has disappeared, and we have reason to believe Vasklin has her."

Vin's watery eyes bored into him. "Then it is you who have my sympathy. And my word as a gentleman I will not rest until she is safe in your arms."

"You would do this for me? A stranger? And a half-breed?"

"What does the color of your skin have to do with anything?" Vin responded. "I would do this for anyone."

Zach gazed at those in front and those behind and a constriction formed in his throat. He tried to shrug it off by telling himself that each one had a personal reason for being there, but the fact remained that they were willing to help him with no thought to the outcome.

When this was over, if he lived, he had a lot of serious thinking to do.

# Chapter
# Fourteen

Dawn was only an hour away. For the most part, the city lay quiet under a speckled mantle of stars. The Regal Club was still open; it stayed open all night. But only a few carriages were out front and the three men on the stoop were struggling to stay awake.

Duncan had insisted on stopping at his apartment on their way there. Not for himself, but for Zach and Alain. "They won't let the two of you back in the door if they recognize you. So we must ensure they don't. I will lend each of you some of my clothes."

Alain only needed a frock coat and a wide-brimmed hat to disguise himself. Zach needed an entire change of wardrobe. He had to admit, as he studied himself in a mirror, that with a frock coat and striped pants instead of his buckskins and with his hair tied back and the hat Duncan had given him, he could pass for a gambler.

Now, standing in the recessed entryway to a butcher shop, Zach listened to Duncan's final instructions.

"We'll go in pairs at two-minute intervals. That way most of us will be inside before they suspect, if they do." He rattled off the names of those who would go together.

Zach expected to be matched with Alain but Duncan took Alain with him; they went first, and everyone watched expectantly as they neared the entrance. The guards hardly glanced at de Fortier.

"It worked!" Fontaine said.

Vin nodded. "Duncan's plans always work."

Zach wished he shared their confidence. He had been paired with Thorne, and they were next. Smoothing his frock coat, which fit loosely about his shoulders and waist, he headed for the club.

"Stay behind me with your head down," Thorne advised. "If they don't get a good look at your face we should be all right."

"I have not had the chance to thank you for your help," Zach said.

"I'm not doing this for you, boy. I'm doing it for Duncan. He's my best friend, and in my line of work, friends are as rare as a royal flush." Thorne chuckled. "That, and I do so love a good scrape. There's nothing quite like the prospect of having one's brains blown out to get the blood flowing."

Zach had known a few Shoshone warriors like him, warriors who lived for the thrill of counting coup. He was once one of them.

"When the shooting starts, find your sister and leave the rest to us," Thorne whispered. "After tonight there will be one less gambling hall and a lot less scum."

By then they were near The Regal Club and Zach dared not speak. Two of the three ruffians were sitting down. The third was picking his teeth with a sliver of wood. "Evening, gentlemen," he said.

"Are we too late to sit in on a game?" Thorne asked.

"It's never too late at the Regal," the man said. "From dusk until dawn, every night of the year."

"So we hear." Thorne held the door for Zach.

Zach did not look up until they were halfway to the bar. The club had thinned out. There were only half as many as before. No one paid any attention to him. Across the room were Alain and Duncan, observing a poker game.

"What would you like to drink?" Thorne asked. "It's on me."

"Nothing." Zach had never been fond of liquor. It befuddled his head and left him with pounding headaches.

Thorne ordered Scotch. He regarded the dirty glass with disdain and wiped the rim clean with his sleeve. "With all the money he makes, you would think Vasklin could afford to hire competent help."

Zach was scouring every table, every face, but there was no sign of the club's owner. He must be in the rear, Zach figured, and couldn't wait to get back there to search for Evelyn.

The front door opened and in came Richard and Owen. Richard put his handkerchief to his nose and rolled his eyes. Owen said something that caused Richard to titter.

A woman strolled toward Zach. The same woman who had tried to steal Alain's poke. She smiled seductively, if wearily, and said in a throaty whisper, "Care to buy a girl a drink?"

"Some other time," Zach said. "I'm only here to gamble." He thought that would suffice but he had forgotten how persistent her kind could be.

"What's the matter? Don't you like what you see? I've never had a complaint, I'll have you know." She leaned on his shoulder and ran a red fingernail along his ear. "Do me this favor. I've got my quota to think of."

"Quota?" Zach said.

"Hell, yes. I don't meet it, I get beat with a switch. So buy me a drink and we'll go in the back and fool around a little and then you can gamble to your heart's content." Suddenly her green eyes became slits. "Hold on. Don't I know you from somewhere?"

"No."

"Are you sure? I'm positive I've seen you before but I can't remember where. Help me out."

"I have only been in New Orleans a short while," Zach said, "and I would remember someone as pretty as you."

Her grin was as insincere as her interest. "Pretty, am I? All the more reason to treat me to that drink."

Zach had never met so many forward women in his life as those in New Orleans. What did it take, he wondered, to get them to leave him alone?

That was when Thorne turned and jabbed a finger in her face. "Get lost, bitch, before I slap you silly."

"I'd like to see you try!" she huffed, but she left, swearing a streak a river rat would envy.

"Would you really hit her?" Zach asked.

"Not hard, no," Thorne said, and laughed.

In walked Fontaine and Vin. Fontaine drifted toward Duncan and Alain; Vin came toward the bar.

"Only Quinton left," Thorne said. "Then we light the wick."

Zach just happened to glance toward the back as Martin Vasklin and five swaggering toughs came out the back and headed for the front door. Vasklin was leaving! He tried to think of a way to stop him but someone beat him to it.

"Martin!" Duncan yelled. "Still fleecing your customers out of their hard-earned money, I see?"

Alain had disappeared, and Fontaine had taken his place. Richard and Owen were also nearby, Richard fluttering his handkerchief in the air and going on about something or other.

As for Vasklin, he did not hide his surprise at seeing the man who had slain his brother. "You!" He darted a hand under his jacket, then smiled shiftily and drew it out again. "This is indeed a day of unusual events. Welcome, Duncan. Perhaps you would do me the honor of playing against me in a game of chance?"

"Pick your poison," Duncan said.

Vasklin barked orders. Within seconds a table was cleared and two chairs placed across from one another. Sinking into one, he accepted a deck of cards. "What do you say to poker? You can deal if you don't trust me."

"I don't." Gasps attended Duncan as he walked over and claimed his seat. "Just as I never trusted your brother."

Zach sidled nearer so he could catch everything they said, although not so near that Vasklin would notice him.

The insults were having an effect. Martin Vasklin was livid. "Have you forgotten where you are?" he snapped. "This is my club. You know what they say about bating a lion in its den."

Duncan smiled. "Show me the lion."

Vasklin was not amused. He handed the deck over, saying, "I would not want to rush this. These are moments to be savored. To be honest, I can't quite think what to make of you."

More of Vasklin's toughs came out of the back. Others were moving to put themselves between Duncan and the front door. Still others filtered through the onlookers to be closer to their employer and ready to protect him.

Duncan calmly began shuffling. "Is five card stud to your liking?"

"It's as good as any. What stakes are we betting for?"

"Bragging rights," Duncan said.

"I was hoping for more." Vasklin responded. "We have been leading up to this for a long time, you and I."

"Oh?" Duncan said, expertly rifling the cards.

"You and your airs," Vasklin said. "Always so honorable. So noble. Always making yourself out to be better than everyone else."

"Only better than those who taint my profession. Those who cheat by any means they can. Those who have no honor." Duncan stared pointedly at his enemy.

"I give you these final moments," Vasklin said mockingly. "Your arrogance has earned you that much."

"Think so?" Duncan finished shuffling and slapped the deck down between them. "Cut."

Vasklin separated half the deck and put the bottom half on top of the top half. "Doesn't it bother you that you live by a code no one else believes in? You always play fair. You always deal straight, never from the bottom of the deck. You never keep a card up your sleeve. You never use the tricks every gambler in New Orleans uses."

"Not all of them," Duncan said, taking the top card and sliding it face down across the table. "Some place a higher value on integrity than winning. It is why I am admitted to the finer gambling houses and you are not."

"Kitty has never refused me entry to her place."

"She gives everyone the benefit of the doubt. But the day you are caught cheating under her roof will be the day she bans you." Duncan placed a card in front of him. "Name any other reputable house where you are welcome. The Royale? The Levee House? The gaming rooms at any of the best hotels?"

Vasklin colored slightly. "I'm not accepted because I wasn't born with a silver spoon in my mouth. It's as simple as that."

"Your kind always use that as an excuse," Duncan said. "You refuse to admit your own shortcomings but are always quick to point out shortcomings in others."

"What do you know?" Vasklin's sneer was laced with savage contempt. "You are no different than they."

"That's where you're wrong," Duncan said. "They would never soil themselves as I am about to."

"It must be nice to be so sure of yourself," Vasklin said. "To think you are above the common herd."

Zack was wondering how much longer the sparring would go on. Fontaine, he noticed, was only a few feet from Duncan's chair, his hand under his frock coat. And now Thorne was moving toward them but acting disinterested.

Vasklin saw Fontaine. "I see you have brought a friend along tonight."

"Many friends," Duncan said.

Vasklin gazed about the room and abruptly stiffened. He did not like what he saw. "My club is rarely graced with so many of your brotherhood. Quinton I would recognize anywhere with that white head of his." Vasklin gave a tiny start. "Is that Vin Connors by the bar?"

"One and the same," Duncan said, dealing the last of their cards. "He wouldn't miss this for all the gold ever mined. Something to do with his sister, I believe."

Worry ate at Vasklin's features but he adopted a casual smile. "If one did not know better, one would think you were the general of an invading army."

"I could not have put it better," Duncan said.

Vasklin had it, then. The full import dawned, and he gripped the arms of his chair until his knuckles were white. "Surely you can't be serious? It's four to one."

"Three to one is more like it," Duncan said. "But you know gamblers. Bucking odds is our stock in trade." He raised his cards just high enough to read them. "How many would you like?"

"Eh?" Vasklin said, confused, but only momentarily. He examined his cards and slid three to the center of the table.

"Three it is." Duncan dealt them. "The dealer takes one." He made a show of taking it from the top, another subtle insult that wasn't lost on those who watched. "What do you have?"

Vasklin did not answer right away. He was gnawing on his lower lip. The impression he presented was that of a rat caught in a trap desperately seeking a way out. "Have what?" he absently asked.

"Your hand," Duncan prodded. "Bragging rights, remember? Are you going to show your cards?"

"Oh." Vasklin turned them over. He had two pair, eights and jacks.

"Not bad," Duncan said. "Not good enough, but not bad." He turned his over one at a time to reveal four kings. "One of us is on a lucky streak tonight."

"It need not come to this," Vasklin said. "I forgave you long ago for my brother."

"No, you haven't," Duncan flatly replied. "You'll never forgive me as long as you live. You'll never stop fleecing everyone who visits your club, never stop what goes on in the back rooms. Not until you are dead." He stated the last with finality.

"Start something and I am not the only one who will die."

"Again you forget you are dealing with gamblers. To us, some rewards are worth the risk. In this instance, it's the reward of removing a blight on the city. That blight being you."

"I should have killed you long ago."

"You were always welcome to try," Duncan said, "but you never were all that brave without your brother to back you. He had most of the courage in your family. And even though he was a cheat, he died like a man. Will you do the same?"

"Go to hell."

"I imagine we both will." Duncan's smile was ice and fire combined. "There's nothing left to be said then, is there? Would you like to start the dance or shall I?"

# Chapter Fifteen

In the silence that greeted Duncan's challenge, Zach King heard the soft rasp of wood on metal and saw Vin Connors twisting his cane. The reason became clear when the handle separated from the sheath to reveal a gleaming sword.

Nearly everyone in the club was now aware that ominous thunderheads of violence loomed. All those playing cards and faro had stopped, all the talk had died, and almost all eyes were on Duncan and Martin Vasklin. The former sat relaxed and self-assured; the latter seemed stunned by the gauntlet hurled in his face.

"You can't just waltz into a man's place of business and threaten his life," Vasklin blustered. "You complain about my lack of breeding when you're no better."

"Do you really want me to recite a litany of your evil?" Duncan responded. "We would be here for a week."

"Your humor is not appreciated."

Duncan's voice acquired a flinty edge. "I will offer you a way out, if only to spare those who might take a stray bullet. Meet me at noon at Potter's Field. Bring seconds, if you like, so long as they abide by the rules of conduct."

"A duel? With you?" Vasklin's laugh was brittle. "Wasn't killing my brother enough?"

"I never had anything against him personally. His mistake in life was looking up to you. In thinking you were worthy of respect."

Hatred twisted Vasklin's features. "Some insults are not to be borne."

"Then give the word. Or are you too spineless?"

Vasklin's men were eager, if he wasn't. Many had knives half drawn, pistols half revealed. They were waiting for their boss to give the command before committing themselves.

An exodus was underway toward the front door. No one wanted a part in the impending melee, and Zach didn't blame them.

Fontaine stepped to Duncan's side. "This is getting ridiculous. Since he won't and you can't, permit me." And with that, Fontaine drew a pistol from under his frock coat, pointed it at one of Vasklin's lieutenants, and blew the top of the man's head off, spattering hair, blood and brains over everyone within a ten-foot radius.

For a few seconds no one moved. The body melted to the floor oozing brain and grisly gore. Patrons were aghast. One woman put a hand over her mouth, about to be sick. Martin Vasklin shook as if with the ague, his face growing redder and redder until something inside of him snapped and he threw back his head and shrieked, "Kill them! Kill them all!"

Hell was unleashed. Amid the screams and yells of bystanders, the club boomed to the blast of gunfire and the harsh metallic clang of forged steel.

Everything happened so fast. Zach saw a pistol appear in Duncan's right hand but before Duncan could fire, Vasklin upended the table and kicked it, sending it crashing over. Duncan nimbly pushed it aside and leaped to his feet but by then Vasklin had ducked in among the panicked bystanders. Instead, Duncan shot one of Vasklin's men who was fixing a bead on his chest.

Everywhere it was the same, violence run rampant. Thorne flicked his wrists and derringers blossomed in each hand. He shot a man on his right, another charging at him from the left. Fontaine was grappling with two adversaries. Quinton had produced a big knife and was laying about him with bloody mastery. Richard and Owen were swapping shots with ruffians at the bar.

Vin Connors had drawn his sword cane and was making for Martin Vasklin. Several of Vasklin's underlings tried to stop him and fell to the glittering tapestry of steel he so adroitly wove. He was an exceptional swordsman—parry, thrust, counter, slash; he cut a swath through them like a reaper through a field of wheat.

Zach absorbed all this in the opening instants of the conflict. Then there was no time to observe, no time to think, no time for anything other than staying alive as three men rushed him. A pistol went off and sent his hat flying. He answered with his own, dropping one would-be killer and then another. The third sliced a dagger at his throat but he skipped aside. Shoving both spent pistols under his belt, he jerked out his bowie, barely blocking the next swing.

The man dropped into a crouch and shifted his dagger from one hand to the other. "I remember you, breed," he hissed. "We should have killed you earlier." It was an oversight he sought to remedy by pivoting on the ball of his left foot and stabbing at Zach's jugular.

Zach's arm moved in pure reflex. He swatted the dagger aside and twisted to avoid another stab, down low. His bowie was huge compared to the dagger but it was heavier and not as easily wielded, a weakness the cutthroat exploited by unleashing a furious flurry intended to sweep past his guard and swiftly end their fight. But the man did not know that Zach had been using a knife since he was old enough to hold one. He did not know that Zach had been in knife fights before, that Zach had practiced and practiced until the bowie was an extension of his hand, until its size was of no consequence.

Sneering confidently, the man feinted, then drove his dagger at Zach's neck. It was a killing stroke but one that never landed. Slipping in close, Zach avoided the lethal sting of the double-edge blade while simultaneously burying his bowie between the man's ribs. He felt the blade scrape bone, felt the flesh give of tissue and organs, felt warm, damp drops on his hand.

The man grunted and looked down at himself, at the blood staining his shirt. More dribbled from the corners of his mouth. "I'll be damned," he bubbled, and his knees caved. He was dead before he struck the floor.

Zach whirled. The club was a madhouse of shooting, screaming, dying. Clouds of gunsmoke were thicker than fog.

Over by the upturned table, Duncan and Thorne were involved in knife fights of their own. Quinton's cadaverous frame was at the thick of a roiling wave of fierce combat. Vin Connors was ringed by five assailants, three of them armed with swords, and was a marvel to behold; his sword cane was living lightning. But he could not withstand such overwhelming odds for long, and Zach moved to help him.

Someone beat him to it. Out of the riot of confusion bounded Alain, his sword dripping scarlet drops, his shirt ripped, his cheek nicked, his face aglow with the excitement and thrill. He disposed of one of Vin's antagonists without breaking stride, and then he and Vin were shoulder to shoulder, blade to blade.

Zach reached them just as they closed with the remaining four. A man with a sword spun toward him and thrust at his heart. By the sheerest of fractions he deflected it, and then had to retreat under an onslaught

the likes of which he had never been pitted against.
Pain seared his left bicep. His right thigh was cut. Par-
rying and blocking, he retreated until his back collided
with the bar.

The man paused, wagging his weapon in a circle.
"Any last words?" he asked, and lunged.

It was hard to say who was more surprised by what
occurred next; a shot cracked and the man's temple exploded, with one eye popping from its socket. His
mouth moved soundlessly as he keeled over.

Ten yards away, leaning on a table, was Fontaine, the
front of his white shirt bright red. He nodded at Zach,
and smiled.

Zach returned the gesture, then plunged back into
the thick of things. A scruffy tough had reloaded and
was bringing a flintlock to bear on Alain's back. Taking
a long bound, Zach cleaved his skull from crown to ear.
The gun never went off.

By now bodies littered the floor. Many had given up
the ghost. Many others were thrashing in agony or
moaning and whimpering. A man who had lost a hand
pressed the stump to his chest and howled. Another
whose neck spurted a fine red mist was rolling back and
forth in blubbering hysterics.

The front door was wide open and a few last customers were fleeing into the night.

Zach turned and saw Owen go down, a knife through
his side. Almost immediately Richard was there, wreak-
ing vengeance.

Several hirelings had sought cover behind the bar and were firing as quickly as they could reload. One raised up to shoot only to have a goodly portion of his face blown away by a well-placed shot from Duncan.

Ducking, Zach raced to the rear. There was probably a back way out, and the girls might take the opportunity to flee, Evelyn among them. He was a few steps from the hall when out of it hurtled a bearded slab of muscle who was also armed with a bowie, and who, the split-second they saw each other, snarled like a grizzly and sought to remove Zach's head from his shoulders.

Zach brought his blade up in time but the blow nearly wrenched the knife from his grasp. He evaded another swing, then backpedaled. The man was on him before he could take three steps. The glint of the man's bowie was all the forewarning Zach had. Again he countered, again he saved himself but not without cost; the blunt back of his knife slammed into him and bright pinpoints of light swirled before his dazed yes.

Zach braced for the killing stroke sure to come. He was completely at the other's mercy. He had failed his sister, had failed his whole family. There was a yelp and a grunt, and his vision cleared as the man wound up in a lifeless heap.

"Come, *mon ami,*" Alain said, pulling his dripping sword from the body. "We must find your sister."

Zach did not need further encouragement. He was first to the hall. On Mercury's wings he darted from door to door, throwing each open and calling out, "Evelyn! Evelyn! It's me, Zach!" At the fourth room he gaped in shock and horror, struggling to comprehend how one human being could do this to another.

"Why have you stopped?" Alain asked at his elbow, and then shouldered him aside. "Keep searching. I will cut her free."

Zach tried not to think of *that* happening to Evelyn but could not resist a flood of searing images. When they told him Martin Vasklin was wicked, he had no true notion of the depths Vasklin plumbed. This went beyond anything he ever imagined, into a shadow realm inhabited by the sickest of minds.

He didn't bother with the latch to the next door. He kicked the door in, and smiled to reassure a girl cowering in a corner. "I won't hurt you." He started out but she lowered her hands and called out to him.

"Wait! Who are you? What is all the shooting about?"

"The man who forced you to stay here is dead," Zach said. Or so he hoped. "You're free to go."

"Go where?" was her timid reply. "I don't have any folks. I don't have family of any kind except Mr. Vasklin."

"You'll find someone." Zach did not have time for this; he had half the rooms to check yet. She yelled for him to wait but he ran to the next door and shoved it wide. The room was empty, but on the floor lay a rawhide whip and manacles.

Zach would dearly love to strangle the life from Martin Vasklin with his own two hands. Or better yet, stake him out over an ant hill after peeling off his skin. Some people did not deserve to live.

Alain had been checking the rooms on the other side. Now he reappeared, pushing two girls aged fourteen or fifteen ahead of him. "*Ici.* There is something you should hear."

The girls were frightened and clung to one another as if expecting to be shot. "Leave us be!" the skinniest cried. "We haven't done anything!"

"Tell my friend what you just told me," Alain directed.

The skinny one raised her face to Zach. "He says you're looking for a girl named Evelyn, is that right?"

"Yes," Zach said, his breath catching in his throat.

"There's a new girl here by that name. I've talked to her a couple of times, but I don't know where she is now."

Zach couldn't help himself; he gripped her shoulders. "You must have some idea! Where can I find her?"

"You're squeezing too hard," the girl said, wresting free. "When the shooting started, everyone started running every which way. I don't know where she got to."

Fear seized him. Zach sprinted from room to room bawling Evelyn's name but there was no answer. The last door was to the outside, and it was open. A block away a small figure was running for dear life. "Wait!" he hollered, about to go after her. Then he noticed how she was running, with short, clipped steps. Evelyn had the long loping gait of an antelope. It wasn't his sister.

Alain still had hold of the pair in the hall. "You ran off without hearing the rest," he said.

"What else is there?" Zach's emotions were in a jumble. He did not know what to do next.

The skinny girl answered. "Mr. Vasklin might have taken her away. He has a house where he keeps a few girls for himself. The girls who catch his fancy. He's never told me where it is."

She had more to say but Zach did not stay to hear it. Rage filled him. Boundless, roiling, total rage. It was the same way he felt that night months ago when he slew Athena Borke's brother, Artemis, at the trading post, and again later when he slit Phineas's throat. It propelled him down the hall and out into the main room.

The Regal Club was a shambles. Tables and chairs had been knocked over, table legs and chairs had been shattered. Chips and money and glasses littered the floor. So did spreading pools of blood from dozens of dead and dying. The sickly sweet smell of it was enough to make weaker stomachs gag.

Duncan was by the bar, cradling Fontaine's head on his leg. He looked up and sadly shook his head. Further off lay Owen, dead; Richard openly weeping over him. Quinton and Thorne had both been wounded but were on their feet. Vin was untouched but soaked in the blood of those he had slain.

Zach was sorry for their loss. Truly sorry. But only one thing was on his mind. "Martin Vasklin?"

Duncan scowled. "The weasel got away in all the confusion. He could be anywhere by now."

The news deflated Zach as if he were a punctured water skin. They had accomplished nothing. Two of them slain, and for what? How many others had died, to what end? The polecat responsible for it all was gone, and Evelyn was still in his clutches.

Zach closed his eyes and groaned.

# Chapter Sixteen

"I don't understand why no one has come," Zach commented. Fifteen minutes had gone by and the authorities had not appeared.

"They are not paid enough to brave a hail of bullets," Thorne said, while having his arm bandaged by Vin. "We don't need them butting in, anyway."

"They won't show up until after sunrise," was Quinton's opinion. He lay on the bar, Duncan busily tending his four wounds.

"This one in your side is serious. You need a doctor. Thorne will take you to the hospital."

"Me?" Thorne pulled away from Vin and Vin pulled him back again. "Why do I have to go?"

"You're wounded, too," Duncan said. "The rest of us only have nicks and cuts."

"I don't like being left out."

"Would you rather Quinton died?" Duncan demanded. "I think he's bleeding inside, and a sawbones can do a lot better job of sewing him up than I can."

Alain was helping himself to some brandy, chugging it straight from the bottle. Richard was on his knees beside Owen's bloodstained body, clasping Owen's hand.

Duncan started toward them but stopped beside one of Vasklin's henchmen who had taken a slug high in the chest and was lying on his back, whining. "What have we here?" Duncan nudged him and the man cried out.

"Don't! I hurt! God, I hurt!"

Bending, Duncan examined the wound. "Looks like you don't have very long to live, so you'd better talk fast." He gripped the man's stubbly chin. "I'm going to ask you a question. I will only ask once. If you don't tell me what I want to know, the pain you are feeling now will be nothing compared to the pain you will feel when I am done with you."

"Please," the man whimpered.

"Where does Martin Vasklin live?"

"How the hell should I know? He's never told me. I work for him, is all." The man groaned. "Haven't you done enough? Go away."

"I warned you," Duncan said, and stomped on the wound.

A howl of anguish rose to the ceiling. The man tried to sit up but couldn't with Duncan's foot pinning him.

"Stop! Don't! I can't stand it!"

"Your employer's address," Duncan said. "We know he has girls there, and we mean to find them."

"What are they to you?" the man asked, then shrieked when Duncan applied more pressure. "Damn you! Damn you all to hell! I'll never tell, do you hear me? Not in a million years!"

Zach's legs were in motion before he knew what he was going to do. Drawing the bowie, he stood over the coward. "Permit me," he said to Duncan, and squatted. "Vasklin has my sister."

The whites of the man's eyes showed. "What's that to me? I have nothing to do with the girls. None of us are allowed anywhere near them."

"Tell me where he lives."

"What I told your friend goes double for you!" the man defied him. "I don't care what you want, and I don't care about your stinking sister."

"I do. His address," Zach said.

"No! No! No!"

"You do not hear very well," Zach said. "So I guess you have no use for this." He swung the knife in a glittering arc.

An ear plopped to the floor, tufts of hair still attached. The man opened his mouth to scream, but no sound came out. He began to tremble as blood seeped between his fingers and down his neck.

"Where?" Zach said, raising his arm to strike again.

"No! No! I'll tell you! Dear God in heaven, I'll tell you. Just don't cut me again." He gave them the address.

"Thank you," Zach said, and sank the bowie into his chest. He held on as the body flopped and kicked and gradually subsided, then he wiped the blade clean on the man's shirt, and stood. Everyone was staring at him. "What?"

"Nothing," Duncan said.

"I put him out of his misery," Zach said to justify his deed.

"I would have done the same," Vin said.

It was plain some of the others disagreed. Thorne, in particular, looked vexed, but he didn't say anything as Duncan and Vin helped Quinton to stand and Quinton slipped a thin arm over Thorne's broad shoulders.

"Off you go," Duncan said. "We'll come to the hospital after our business with Vasklin is finished."

Thorne tried one more time. "I don't like leaving you. Can't someone else take him? Vin, how about you?"

"I trust you are joking."

"Richard?"

"Do you have eyes? Do you see what they did to Owen? I won't rest until every last one of the bastards has met his Maker."

Duncan clapped Thorne on the back. "There you have it. Off you go. Fremont Street is one block over and you can usually find a cab there, even at this hour." He clasped Quinton's hand. "Thank you."

"I wouldn't have missed it for the world," the white-haired giant grinned. "Next time, though, I'm bringing a brace of pistols, two rifles and a cannon." He laughed at his joke, or tried to, and had a coughing fit.

"Get going," Duncan urged Thorne, and saw them to the door.

Zach had come to a decision. Clearing his throat to get their attention, he announced, "I'm grateful for your help." He truly was. He could not get over that these strangers, *white* men, no less, had risked their lives to aid someone they only just met. "But I do not want any more of you to die." Fontaine and Owen were two more lives chalked up to Athena Borke's account. "I will go it alone from here."

"Like hell you will," Vin said. "You're not the only one whose sister has been snared in Vasklin's net. I'll see this through to the end, and nothing you can say will stop me."

"I, too, *mon ami*," Alain said.

"It's not necessary," Zach replied. "You have repaid me for saving your life many times over."

The Creole shrugged. "I have come this far, eh? I would be less of a man were I to leave you in the lurch now."

Richard had come over and was wiping his tear-moistened cheeks with his sleeve. "Don't even think of leaving me out. I'll shoot you if you do."

That left Duncan. His handsome face streaked with black powder residue and spattered with red drops, his body bearing the mark of a dozen minor hurts, he said, "Fontaine was like a brother to me. I have a blood debt of my own to settle now."

The first faint hint of dawn tinged the eastern horizon as the five of them wound along the narrow streets. Here and there an early riser sat on a patio or a balcony and watched them go by.

Zach was mired in thought. Now that he knew beyond any shade of doubt that Evelyn had been at the club, his heart was heavy with sorrow. She had always been the sweetest of creatures, the most innocent of innocents. Because of Vasklin, her purity had been perverted, her soul marked forever by his taint. For that alone Vasklin must die the most horrible of deaths. No quick mercy for him. Zach would make sure Martin Vasklin suffered as few men ever had.

Torture was not new to him. It was a common practice among some tribes to torture captured enemies. Not out of cruelty, nor from a depraved desire to see others suffer, but to test a captive's mettle. The Shoshones did not indulge in the practice that often, but when they did, they were every bit as thorough as the Crows or the Sioux or the Blackfeet.

When he was six, Zach happened to be staying with his folks at Touch The Clouds's village when a Piegan raiding party tried to steal some horses but was driven away. In the fight, two boys tending the herd were slain. Not long after, one of the Piegans took an arrow in the leg and was captured.

Zach still remembered holding his mother's hand, watching, horror-struck, as the Piegan's stomach was slit open and his intestines were unwound like a spool of thick, pulpy thread. He remembered the Piegan's tongue being cut out. Remembered the grandmother of one of the slain boys taking off the Piegan's pants and doing something that to this day sent a shiver down his spine. Other things, too, terrible, terrible things, never to be talked about for as long as he lived. Yet the Piegan never cried out, never pleaded for his life. That Piegan was an enemy, but he died as a warrior should and in doing so earned the respect of every Shoshone there.

That was the first time. There were others. Atrocities Zach witnessed that would sicken most whites. He had seen the Sioux skin a soldier alive and stake him out under the burning sun, then gouge out his eyes. He had seen what was left of a party of Mexicans after Apaches mutilated them. And more. So much more.

Violence was a daily part of life on the frontier. Brutal acts were committed as a matter of course; a grizzly ripped an unwary warrior to pieces, Comanches honed their skill with their lances on a prisoner tied to a tree, a pack of wolves brought down a frightened fawn. It was the cycle of life in all its violent splendor.

Everyone who lived west of the Mississippi, every frontiersman and Indian, knew that one day he might be called on to endure the horror of horrors. No one complained. No one railed in protest to the heavens. It was the nature of things. It had always been the nature of things. It would always be the nature of things. To rail at violence was to rail at life, and where was the sense in that?

Zach had learned that most whites did not share that view. Most avoided dwelling on the unthinkable. They tried to deny death existed by shutting it from their minds. But death was never truly denied, never truly held at bay. Death always had the last word, for the basic and inescapable reason that all life ended in death.

All Zach asked was that his own death be delayed long enough for him to save Evelyn and avenge himself on Athena Borke.

Suddenly Duncan broke their long silence, saying, "Life is full of surprises. The Regal Club must be more lucrative than I imagined if Vasklin can afford to live here."

Zach looked around. He had taken it for granted that a despicable pile of dung like Vasklin lived in the worst section of the city, but such was not the case. Fine homes graced both sides of an oak-lined street. Every home had a garden shaded by magnolias and a wide front porch. "Where are we?"

"The Garden District," Vin said. "Americans live here mostly. Well-to-do Americans, I should say."

"I have friends here," Richard remarked. He had been uncharacteristically quiet since his friend's passing.

"Vasklin always has wanted to rub elbows with the upper crust," Duncan said. "He likes to pretend he's one of them."

"We all have our pretensions," Richard commented.

"*Mon Dieu.* Are you defending him?" This from Alain.

"Never in a million years," Richard said. "He's a rabid cur who needs to be disposed of once and for all."

"On that we could not agree more," Alain said. "I have met many despicable excuses for human beings in my time, but none can hold a candle to this one."

Around them quiet reigned. The Garden District had not yet stirred to life to greet the imminent dawn.

A dog barked at them and was hushed by its owner. A man came out on his porch in a robe and at sight of them hastily went back inside. A woman peered at them from a window and Alain blew her a kiss.

Duncan was reading house numbers. "We're close," he informed them. "It should be just ahead if I'm not mistaken."

Alain stopped. "Perhaps we should take a moment to dedicate ourselves to our cause." He held a fist out at chest height. "I vow to give my life, if need be, in our noble cause."

Zach did not see the point. They were already determined to see it through. But he went along with the rest and held a fist out.

"To vengeance," Alain swore. "May none of us give up or turn back until we have done what we came here to do."

"I second that," Duncan said.

"You needn't worry on my account," Vin declared, brandishing his sword cane. "My blade has not drunk enough blood."

"I will see it through, too," said Richard.

Without anyone suggesting they should, they spread across the street. Zach was on the right, and as it turned out, so was Vasklin's house. Painted white with black shutters, it was flanked by willows. Roses bordered the porch. It was a perfect home in a perfect neighborhood.

"Can this really be it?" Alain marveled.

Zach was alert for dogs but did not see any. Nor were there any guards. Like Alain, he had his doubts.

Five abreast, they warily crossed the lawn. No angry shouts greeted them. No shots blasted.

"It can't be this easy," Duncan said.

"Perhaps we were lied to," Richard replied.

Zach swore under his breath. The cutthroat at the club had been braver than he thought. He was about to say that he, too, thought they must have the wrong house, when suddenly every ground floor window was smashed to bits by rifle barrels thrust from inside, and above the din rose the sadistically gleeful shout of Martin Vasklin, yelling what he had yelled back in his club:

"Kill them! Kill them all!"

# Chapter
# Seventeen

Vasklin's impatience cost him. Had he waited until they climbed the steps, Zach and his allies would have been shot where they stood. But as it was, they were at the bottom of the steps, and when the windows dissolved in showers of shimmering shards, they did what anyone else would have done: They threw themselves to the ground.

A ragged volley spewed hot lead and acrid smoke but not one shot scored.

Zach was instantly on his knees, a pistol in each had. The Hawken was at Duncan's apartment since he couldn't very well have carried it into the club. Not that he needed it. At close range pistols were just as effective, as he proved with two swift shots that spun one rifleman around and punched another from a window.

The others were firing: Duncan, Alain, Richard and Vin peppered the ground floor.

Zach could not say how many assassins were inside, but it was a safe guess that once again he and the others were outnumbered. Dropping down, he swiftly reloaded. Inside the house Vasklin was bellowing, but Zach could not quite make out what he was shouting about.

With a loud tinkling of glass, a window on the upper floor shattered and a rifleman sighted down at them, aiming at Richard.

"Down!" Duncan yelled, and fired from the hip. He was as skilled a marksman as he was at cards.

The rifleman pitched out the window and dangled half in and half out, spilling what was left of his brains on the porch eaves.

Zach was watching the windows but no more shooters appeared. He glimpsed a silhouette and took a swift bead but it vanished.

Then Alain whispered his name. "Maybe it is better if we hold our fire and ask for a truce."

"Why would we want to do that?" Zach responded. Personally, he did not intend to rest until Vasklin was dead at his feet.

"Your sister, eh?"

To Zach it was like a slap in the face. How could he forget Evelyn? She might be hit by a stray slug. He glanced at the others; Duncan nodded; Richard shook his head; Vin mouthed, "Yes."

Zach faced the house. "Vasklin! Can you hear me in there?"

"My ears work fine, breed!" came the angry reply. "What will it take to be rid of you?"

"I want my sister!" Zach shouted. "Send her out unharmed and we will go away without firing another shot."

Richard swore, then growled, "Like hell we will. Speak for yourself. I never knew a finer man than Owen Trent and I will not let his killers off the hook."

"Keep your voice down." This from Duncan, who leaned toward Richard to whisper, "I agree with you, but we have the girl to think of. Once she is safe you can do as you please."

After a few moments Richard grumbled, "Go ahead." But he fingered his pistol as if he could not wait to use it.

"Well?" Zach yelled. "What will it be, Vasklin? Spill more blood or be sensible?"

"Does this sister of yours have a name?"

"Evelyn! And don't tell me you don't know her. I know a girl by that name was at your club."

A shadow materialized by a front window, partially screened by drapes. "You're Evelyn's brother? Is that what you would have me believe?"

"Why do you sound so surprised?" Zach returned. "I have come many miles to find her and I will not rest until I do."

"She isn't here."

"I don't believe you." Zach was sure Evelyn was in there. She *had* to be.

"I did not bring any girls with me," Vasklin said. "There was not enough time. And I was thinking more of my skin than theirs."

It was plausible, but Zach refused to accept it. "Then where, if not here? And don't feed me another of your lies."

"Shortly before you and your friends showed up, I sent Evelyn and two other girls to a boathouse I own down by the waterfront. They're to leave at first light to visit a client upriver. One who pays extra for house calls." Vasklin snickered.

Zach's limbs began to tremble. Evelyn was still alive! Soon he would hold her in his arms and assure her that her ordeal was over. "You will take me to her without delay."

"Just the two of us?" Vasklin said.

"If that is how you want it." Zach would do anything, anything at all. "But I keep my weapons."

"And I keep mine?"

"Don't trust him," Duncan said.

Zach was torn between needing Vasklin to agree and common sense. "No. No weapons for you. I would be a fool to trust you."

Martin Vasklin did not like it. "I must think this over. Give me a few minutes."

What is there to think about? Zach almost demanded, but he bit his lip, then said, "Only a few." The shadow disappeared, and Zach hunkered to await the outcome. He would not wait long.

Duncan had thought of something else, and whispered, "I wouldn't put it past him to try and sneak out the back. One of us should work his way around to keep an eye on them."

"I'll go," Richard volunteered.

"You?" Duncan said suspiciously.

"Why not? Do you think I'll go rushing in by myself?" Richard snorted. "I can't take revenge for Owen if I'm dead, now can I?"

"Fair enough," Duncan said, "but I want your word as a gentleman you won't do a thing unless they make a break for it."

"You wound me to the quick, but you have my word." Richard crawled along the bottom step to the corner. Then, keeping a lilac bush between himself and the house, he began circling around.

"I wouldn't have let him go," Alain remarked.

"He's not the one we need to worry about," Duncan said, with a meaningful glance at Vin.

Zach was beginning to think Vasklin would not take him up on it when the shadow reappeared by the window and a hand cracked the drape.

"Breed?"

"I'm here," Zach answered.

"I've talked it over with my men. I will take you to your sister but only under two conditions."

The last thing Zach wanted was for Vasklin to make demands, but so long as they were not delayed in reaching Evelyn, he reasoned it might be best to agree. "Name them and we'll see."

"First, your friends must pull back to the end of the block. That includes the one who just snuck around back. I give you my word my men will not shoot."

"Why should they?" Zach snapped. It sounded like another trick.

"Because I see Vin Connors out there, and I know how much he would like to see me dead. I don't come out so long as he is anywhere near the house."

Zach turned to Duncan, who nodded. "We agree. But we have a condition of our own. None of your men can show themselves at the windows until we are out of range."

"Agreed."

"What else?"

"You and I go unarmed. Give your guns and knife to de Fortier and I will leave my weapons here. That's the only way I will trust you not to kill me before we get there."

To Zach the request rang false. Vasklin knew all he cared about was Evelyn, and that he was not about to kill him before they reached her.

"Well?" Vasklin prompted when he did not get a reply. "What will it be, halfblood? Do you want to see her or not?"

Alain slipped a hand into his right boot and drew out a pearl-handled stiletto. "It's not much but it's better than nothing."

Zach accepted it with a grateful smile. Cutting a

whang from his left sleeve, he slid the stiletto up under his sleeve and tied it in place, then lowered his sleeve and gave his arm a tentative shake. The stiletto stayed where it was.

"Some time this year!" Martin Vasklin called.

"I agree!" Zach yelled, and passed his guns and the bowie to Alain.

Richard came crawling back around the lilac bush. "I heard," he said, "and I think you're making a mistake."

With their pistols trained on the windows, Duncan and the rest rose and warily backed across the yard. All up and down the street people were peering from windows and peeking from doorways.

"There!" Zach hollered when the gamblers and Alain were where Vasklin wanted them. "We've held up our end. Now you hold up yours."

The front door opened and Vasklin stepped out, his arms out from his sides, his hands empty. Smirking, he turned completely around. "Satisfied? Now you do the same."

Zach complied, then motioned. "After you."

Vasklin glanced at one of the windows and nodded, then walked to the street. Instead of going down it, he crossed through the next yard to the next street and then turned right. "In case Vin has any ideas about going back on his word," he said.

"He worries you, that one."

"No one has ever hated me as much as he does, and when a man is ruled by hate, he is capable of anything."

Zach surreptitiously fingered the dagger through his sleeve, thinking how much he would love to bury it in Vasklin's heart.

"I must admit, breed, you've proven more of a problem than I counted on," Vasklin said.

"If my sister has been touched I will prove to be even more of one," Zach vowed.

Vasklin chuckled, as if that were humorous. He kept glancing back and did not say anything until he was sure they were not being followed. "Well, it looks like Duncan's bunch did as they were told."

"Duncan is an honorable man."

"Too honorable," Vasklin spat. "He expects everyone to live by the same code he does. He had no right to challenge my brother to that duel over something as trifling as cheating. Hell, I cheat all the time, and no one has ever challenged me."

"Only because they have never caught you at it." Zach had heard this from Thorne earlier.

"Go to hell," Vasklin said. "In your way, you're as bad as he is. All this aggravation you've caused me, and for what? Because I run a business."

Zach's temper flared. "Is that what you call it? Forcing those girls to do what they do?"

"I fill a need. People crave what I offer. Blame those willing to pay, don't blame me."

It took every iota of self-control Zach possessed not to kill Vasklin then and there. "And whites call my people savage and primitive," he remarked.

"Apples and oranges, breed. Apples and oranges. Your

heathen ways aren't our ways and our ways aren't yours."

"I would not want them to be." Zach had seen enough white hate and treachery to last a lifetime.

Vasklin had nothing else to say. They left the Garden District and came to an older part of the city where buildings were stacked like cordwood and gardens and trees were rare.

"What tribe do you belong to, anyhow?" Martin Vasklin asked out of the blue.

"The Shoshones," Zach said proudly.

"I've never heard of them. But then, I take after old Andy Jackson. I believe the only good Indian is a dead Indian." Vasklin grinned sadistically.

"There are days when I think the same of most whites," Zach said. Were it not for his wife and his father and uncle and a few friends, he would think the same of *all* whites. Or that's how he used to be. Now, after what Duncan and the others had done for him, he was not so sure.

For some reason Vasklin thought that was funny. "I don't blame your kind for being jealous."

Zach was not sure he had heard correctly. "Jealous of what?"

"Look around you." Vasklin motioned. "This is one of the most modern cities in the country. Paved streets, lamps and stoves in nearly every home, all the conveniences a body could want. Compare that to your kind. I hear tell Indians live in tents made of buffalo hide. That the only light you have is fire. That you starve half the time because you don't have the brains to plant crops. Indians are just as backward as backward can be."

Bristling, Zach had an angry retort on the tip of his tongue but he did not voice it. Something about Vasklin's expression gave him pause. A certain craftiness, a certain glint in Vasklin's beady eyes. It suddenly struck him as strange that Vasklin was going on and on about Indians when Vasklin could not care less about them. It was almost as if Vasklin were doing it deliberately—as if Vasklin wanted to distract him.

At the next corner Zach contrived to glance back when Vasklin wouldn't notice. He saw nothing at first and figured his concern was groundless. Then, a hundred yards distant, a dusky form flitted from one doorway to another. He spied a second farther back, then a third, and a cold rage filled him. Vasklin's men had sneaked out of the house and were shadowing them.

"Another five minutes and we'll be there. What then, breed? Do you take your sister and that's it? We let bygones be bygones?"

"What else?" Zach said, masking his fury.

"That's the first sensible thing you've said since I met you," Vasklin said. "I didn't start this, after all. You did. All I want is for it to be over with. I'm not out for anyone's blood."

"Me either," Zach lied. Before he was done, he would take the lives of this lying dog and all those who worked for him.

"I'm glad you're being so reasonable," Vasklin said. "Soon this will all be over and we can get on with our lives. You have my solemn word." Smiling, he turned— and he was holding a derringer.

# Chapter Eighteen

Tendrils of early morning mist hung over the Mississippi River close to shore. A steamboat chugged downriver, sending thick plumes of smoke from its stacks. Near the dock a large catfish surfaced, then darted down into the depths again.

The boathouse was in need of repair. A flatboat was moored at the dock, half loaded with crates.

Martin Vasklin grinned as they stepped onto the dock. "I can't wait to see the look on your face, breed, when you see your sister. It should be interesting."

"Why?" Zach demanded, his worry over Evelyn flaring anew. Without letting on, he had kept an eye on the two-legged wolves shadowing them, and knew there were five, armed with rifles and pistols. And all he had was the dagger Alain had lent him.

Vasklin was supremely sure of himself. Confidently striding to the boathouse, he knocked loudly. "Open up!"

"Who's there?" someone challenged. "This is private property and we're not to let anyone in."

"It's me, Larson, you idiot," Vasklin said. "Hurry up and open this door before I decide to have you chopped into pieces and fed to the fish."

From the way he said it, Zach had the impression Vasklin was serious, which prompted the thought that Vasklin might have done it to others, and might intend on doing it to him.

A river rat with a crooked, bulbous nose and the broad shoulders of a bull filled the doorway. "Sorry, boss," he said sheepishly. "We weren't expecting you." Behind him were other dangerous men with hard eyes and knives at their hips.

"Bring Evelyn here," Vasklin commanded.

"That little girl, you mean?" Larson asked. "The one with the pretty eyes who has been so nice to me?"

"Who *else* would I mean, you simpleton?"

Larson went back in, but not the three men with him. At a whisper from Vasklin, they moved apart, their hands on their knives. Zach started to back away and heard the soft scuff of a shoe behind him. The five who had been shadowing them were there. He was surrounded with no hope of escape short of fighting his way out, and there were too many for one man to overcome.

Martin Vasklin laughed. "Surprise, surprise. I do so love moments like this. Be honest. Aren't you feeling the least little stupid for trusting me?"

"I had to find out about my sister," Zach said.

"Ah. Yes. Your precious sibling. Here she is now."

Larson's huge bulk emerged first. Holding his hand was a girl no older than fifteen with curly brown hair and a dimpled chin and the tired eyes of all the girls at The Regal Club.

"It's not her," Zach breathed aloud, a lump in his throat, and had it not been for the others, he might have fallen to his knees in heartfelt relief. As it was, he clasped his hands as if in gratitude to the Almighty and looked to the sky, but it was only a pretext for him to slip his right hand up his left sleeve unnoticed.

"It's not?" Vasklin was visibly disappointed. "The hell you say. I was looking forward to doing things to her while you watched."

Zach faced him. "You've lived too long."

"Perhaps I have. I confess life's pleasures have paled of late. I'm too jaded, I suppose, for my own good. But that's what comes from indulging in delights lesser men are afraid to taste."

Tensing every sinew in his body, Zach prepared to spring. One thrust was all he asked. One thrust into the weasel's chest. Then he could die knowing his death was not a waste, even if he had to take the thought of Evelyn still in Athena Borke's clutches with him to his grave.

"Do you want us to shoot him and be done with it,

Mr. Vasklin?" asked a scarred killer holding a cocked pistol.

"And spoil all my fun?" Vasklin rejoined. "I should say not, Bishop. Even without his sister, he still can amuse me. No, I would rather we take him alive. Shoot him in the knee if you must, but only if he resists."

"With pleasure," Bishop said, leering as he took aim. "There's nothing I hate worse in this world than half-breeds—except the filthy Indians who spawn them."

"Wait!" Larson suddenly cried, and pushed the girl named Evelyn through the doorway. "She shouldn't have to see this, boss, young as she is."

"Honestly," Vasklin muttered. "The way you fawn over females and children is positively sickening."

"I'm just being nice," Larson said.

Bishop was itching to squeeze the trigger. "Give the word, Mr. Vasklin, and I'll blow his kneecap off."

Vasklin grinned at Zach. "What will it be, breed? Easy or hard? Frankly, it makes no difference to me."

Zach streaked his right hand from under his sleeve and in the same smooth motion threw it, overhand. The dagger flew straight and true, the keen blade biting deep into the base of Bishop's throat. Bishop bleated like a sheep and took a tottering step, then made the mistake of grabbing the dagger and wrenching it out. Along with it streamed a torrent of red.

Everyone else was momentarily riveted in shock. Vasklin recovered just as Zach leaped at him. "Shoot, damn it! Shoot him dead!"

Several brought their guns to bear but held their fire

for fear of hitting their employer, who met Zach's lunge by seizing Zach's right wrist even as Zach seized his. Locked together, they spun to the right and then the left, Zach striving to wrench Vasklin's arm so he dropped the derringer. Vasklin desperately tried to prevent him from succeeding, all the while shouting, "Shoot! Shoot! Shoot!"

The outcome was a foregone conclusion. At any moment one of the cutthroats would get a clear shot, and that would be that. All Zach could do was hope he had enough life left in him to deliver a fatal stab.

Suddenly Vasklin tripped. Zach slammed a knee into his gut and twisted Vasklin's arm, and the derringer landed at their feet.

"I'll help you, boss!" Larson bellowed, and lumbered to Vasklin's aid. For someone as big as a bull, Larson was exceptionally fast. Before Zach knew it, hands the size of slabs of beef had hold of his arms and were shaking him as a bear might shake a lynx. Against such formidable might Zach was powerless. He was yanked off the ground and swung like a sack of flour against the boathouse. Wood cracked loud in his ears, and his breath left his lungs. Dazed, close to blacking out, Zach raised his head to utter a last cry of defiance.

Zach never voiced it. Figures were darting from the shadows. Three were dressed in black frock coats and one was dressed all in brown.

The pistols in Duncan's hands cracked in cadence and two river rats dropped. Richard shot a third. Vin Connors disdained firearms for his sword cane, slashing right and left. That left Alain de Fortier, who was every bit Vin's equal in swordsmanship and whose flair for the acrobatic was second to none. Springing, whirling, dodging, Alain waded into three of Vasklin's men, his blade everywhere at once.

Zach heard the door slam. Larson and Martin Vasklin were gone. Sucking in a deep breath, he pushed to his feet and opened it. Midway down a long, dark hall were two forms, one huge, one short.

"Stop him!" Vasklin frantically ordered. "Delay him long enough for me to reach the boat!"

"You can count on me, boss," Larson said, planting himself in the middle with his enormous arms and tree trunks legs spread wide.

Zach never hesitated. He charged full speed, giving no thought to being unarmed or to the massive size of the man he faced. Zach ran straight at him, and when he was six feet away, he whipped his legs in front of him as he so often had when he was a boy and liked to slide down dusty mountainsides, and slid between Larson's legs before the dumbfounded giant could think to grab him.

Vasklin was almost to the other end. Rearing erect, Zach sprinted after him. Behind him Larson had turned and was giving chase.

"Dang, you're a slippery cuss!"

Zach had always taken pride in how fast he was. Foot races were popular among the Shoshones, and he had won more than anyone his age except Swift Antelope. Now his fleetness brought him to the far door barely two seconds after Vasklin had gone out. It was swinging shut, and he slammed into it with his shoulder.

A rowboat was tied at the dock, at the foot of a ladder. Vasklin was about to climb down. He whirled at the crash of the door and hissed, "What does it take to stop you?"

Barely breaking stride, Zach covered the final ten feet in a headlong rush and rammed into him. His intention was to knock Vasklin off the dock, and in that he succeeded. But Vasklin got an arm around his neck, and in the blink of an eye he was going over the side, too.

There was the sensation of falling. Zach barely had time to draw air into his lungs before the clammy fist of the muddy river enveloped him, and their combined weight and momentum carried them toward the bottom. A foot struck him in the thigh, a fist caught him in the gut. He felt Vasklin kick free and saw him stroke rapidly for the surface.

Zach rose after him, swimming smoothly, powerfully. He was almost as adept in water as he was at running. They were six or seven feet from the surface when his right hand brushed Vasklin's ankle. Wrapping his fingers tight, he tugged.

Vasklin glanced down, panic in his eyes, his cheeks bulging like those of a chipmunk gathering nuts for the winter. He lashed out with his other foot and whipped his body from side to side.

Zach refused to let go. He could hold his breath for minutes, if need be, more than long enough to end forever Vasklin's depraved stranglehold on New Orleans.

But whatever else he might be, Martin Vasklin was not one to go meekly into eternal night. He kicked harder, pumped his arms harder, and suddenly he was rising again.

Zach swam after him. Stroking cleanly, he broke the surface. Vasklin was pulling himself over the side of the rowboat. *No, you don't!* Zach thought, and clamped his arms around Vasklin's waist. For a few seconds Vasklin resisted, but only a few.

They were underwater again. A thumb gouged Zach in the eye. Fingers dug into his neck. Vasklin was fighting for his life, and he fought dirty. Zach punched him in the gut but the water weakened the blow. Zach closed his right hand on Vasklin's throat but he could not hold on, and once again Vasklin rose out of reach.

This time Vasklin made for the ladder, not the rowboat. He was beginning to climb when Zach reared out of the river and tried to pull him back down.

"Let go, damn you!"

A fist looped at Zach's face. He jerked aside but knuckles scraped his cheek and he almost lost his hold. He punched Vasklin in the back and in the ribs, and received a knee to the jaw that nearly broke his hold and left him dangling. He grabbed at a rung but his wet hand slipped on the wet wood and the next moment a foot to the shoulder sent him plunging into the river.

Zach came up sputtering and shaking his head to clear it and saw Vasklin scrambling up the ladder with the agility of a mountain goat. He also saw Vin, waiting at the top with a pistol in his hand.

Vasklin was looking down and did not realize his fate was sealed. He smirked at Zach, yelled, "I beat you again, breed!" Then he looked up, and froze.

"This is for my sister, you son of a bitch," Vin said, and fired.

The back of Martin Vasklin's skull burst like a rotten melon. Bits of bone and hair flew through the air and into the water. With a loud splash Vasklin's body followed the fragments into the river and sank into oblivion.

Zach continued climbing. Vin lowered a hand to help him, and pulled him up. Duncan and Alain were there, too; Duncan with a pistol on Larson. "The rest are all dead," he said.

"Richard?" Zach asked.

Alain shook his head.

There remained but one more thread to the tapestry.

At Alain's insistence the four of them dined that evening at the most elegant restaurant in New Orleans, The Cockleshell, run by a chef from London. Alain insisted on treating them and was deaf to Duncan and Vin's offer to help pay.

Zach could not offer because he had hardly any money left. It made his glum frame of mind worse. He had failed, failed utterly, and lost Evelyn. Perhaps for good.

He was not paying much attention to what was going on around him, and did not know what to make of it when a pink envelope lavishly scented with perfume was placed in front of him. On the envelope, written in a flowing feminine cursive hand, was: *To Zachary King. For his eyes only.* "What's this?" he asked.

"Courtesy of Harold K. Wilkerson," Alain said. "His manservant handed it to me half an hour ago. Apparently Athena Borke left it on a table in her suite, but none of the hotel staff knew who you were or how to find you." Alain poured himself some wine. "After your antics at his mansion, and after hearing your tale, Wilkerson personally went to the Harvest House to check up on Athena and was given the envelope. He sent it around to me."

"Open it," Duncan urged.

"It must be about your sister," Vin said.

Zach ripped the end of the envelope off and upended it. Out fell a folded pink sheet of stationary. He unfolded it, and blinked in surprise. "This isn't English. It's French." Which he couldn't read.

"May I, *mon ami?*" Alain said, and took the liberty of taking it. "Well now. It seems Miss Borke is fluent in French. Fortunately for you, so am I."

"But why French?" Zach wondered. "Read it, quickly."

"You are sure?" Alain scanned the sheet and his color darkened. Then he read aloud, "*Monsieur Zachary King. If you are reading this, then the traps I have laid have failed and you are still alive. More's the pity, as I have had such fun manipulating you like a puppet. Did you enjoy the game? It is just beginning. For you see, I have decided to broaden your despondent sister's horizons by taking her on a tour of the Continent. That's right. If you want to see her again,*" *alive, you must search for her in Paris, France. By the time you read this we will have set sail. I have been there several times and have many Parisian friends, and I will arrange the warmest welcome for you that you can imagine. My best regards. Athena Borke."*

Vin whistled softly.

"What will you do?" Duncan asked.

"What else can I do," Zach answered, "but somehow scrape up the money to go on to Paris."

Alain de Fortier was thoughtfully swirling the red wine in his glass. "I am long overdue for another visit to France, so what do you say to the two of us going together? And permitting me to pay our way?"

"I couldn't ask that of you. Or anyone." It was more than Zach had any right to expect.

Alain shrugged. "I have nothing better to do. Besides, the excitement, the adventure, they appeal to me. We will save your sister and deal with this Borke woman, and all will be well."

"I hope so," Zachary King said. God, *how* he hoped so!

# JOHN JAKES
# ELMER KELTON
# ROBERT J. RANDISI
### And Others

## The Funeral of Tanner Moody

There's never been a character quite like Tanner Moody. His life was so filled with adventure and drama, it took nine of the West's greatest authors to write about him. In all-original stories, each writer presents a different aspect of Tanner Moody: the lawman, the outlaw, the gunfighter, the man . . . the legend.

As people from far and wide gather for the funeral of Tanner Moody, many have stories to tell, stories from different years of Moody's life, stories that reveal the man they knew, the man they loved, feared, admired . . . or hated. The result is a unique book, a collaboration among nine exciting authors to tell the tale of one exciting life.

----------------------------------------------------

# LANCASTER'S ORPHANS
## Robert J. Randisi

It certainly isn't what Lancaster had expected. When he rode into Council Bluffs, he thought he would just stop at the bar for a beer. How could he know he'd ride right into the middle of a lynching? Lancaster can't let an innocent man be hanged, but when the smoke clears and the lynching stops, a bystander lies dying on the ground, caught in the crossfire. With his last breath he asks Lancaster to take care of the people who had been depending on him—a wagon train filled with women and children on their way to California!

# TOM PICCIRILLI
# Coffin Blues

Priest McClaren wants to put his past behind him. It's a past filled with loss, murder...and revenge. Now all Priest wants is to own a carpentry shop and earn a quiet living building coffins. But it looks like peace and quiet just aren't in Priest's future. His ex-lover has pleaded with him to carry ransom money into hostile territory in Mexico, to rescue her new husband. It's a mission he can't refuse, but it could also easily get him killed. Especially when he runs afoul of Don Braulio, a bandit with a great fondness for knives....

---

**Dorchester Publishing Co., Inc.**
P.O. Box 6640                                          ___5336-5
Wayne, PA 19087-8640                          $5.99 US/$7.99 CAN

Please add $2.50 for shipping and handling for the first book and $.75 for each additional book. NY and PA residents, add appropriate sales tax. No cash, stamps, or CODs. Canadian orders require an extra $2.00 for shipping and handling and must be paid in U.S. dollars. Prices and availability subject to change. **Payment must accompany all orders.**

Name: _____

Address: _____

City: _____ State:_____ Zip: _____

E-mail: _____

I have enclosed $_____ in payment for the checked book(s).

*CHECK OUT OUR WEBSITE!* www.dorchesterpub.com
____ Please send me a free catalog.

# DANE COOLIDGE

# THE WILD BUNCH

Abner Meadows is only trying to get out of the storm when he seeks shelter in the cave. One of the most notorious bandits of the West, Butch Brennan, just happens to be in the same cave...with the loot from his latest holdup. Meadows knows better than to accept Brennan's offer to join his gang, but he is still stuck with the robber's recognizable horse and a few gold pieces.

Back in town, the sheriff raises a posse, and when they catch Meadows on Brennan's horse and then find his double eagles, they're convinced they've got their man. But Meadows will do anything to prove his innocence, including risking his life to track down the wild bunch that framed him.

# GUNS OF VENGEANCE

## LEWIS B. PATTEN

Incessant heat and drought have taken their toll on the Wild Horse Valley range. And nowhere is it worse than on the Double R, the largest ranch in the district, owned by Walt Rand. Things really heat up when Nick Kenyon diverts what little water is left in Wild Horse Creek, giving his little ranch more water than it needs and the Double R none. Kenyon had long since managed to turn all the smaller ranchers against the Double R, blaming Rand and his greed for all the problems on the range. But stealing water in a drought is the last straw, and Rand decides to fight back. He'll deal with Kenyon the same way he would with anyone who stole what belonged to the Double R—with bullets!

---

**Dorchester Publishing Co., Inc.**
P.O. Box 6640                                                    ___5376-4
Wayne, PA 19087-8640                              $4.99 US/$6.99 CAN

# LES SAVAGE, JR.

# WEST OF LARAMIE

Scott Walker returns home to Missouri from his stay in a Confederate hospital only to find his home burned by Quantrill's raiders, and his family relocated to Wyoming. But his long trek to be reunited with his kin is only the beginning of his troubles. When he reaches Laramie he finds his sweetheart married to his older brother, and his father embroiled in a bloody battle with a deputy surveyor for the railroad. Has Scott survived the war only to be killed in a struggle for land? With the railroads on one side, landowners on another, and fierce Indians against them all, Scott is caught in a whirlwind of progress, greed and the efforts to bind a continent with iron rails.

--------------------------------------------------

# THE DEVIL'S CORRAL
# LES SAVAGE, JR.

The three short novels in this thrilling collection are among the finest written by Les Savage, Jr., one of the true masters of Western fiction. The Devil in *The Devil's Corral* is a stubborn horse that has never allowed anyone to ride him. Even worse, Devil puts Ed Ketland in the hospital and gives him a fear of horses, a fear he has to overcome one way or another. *Satan Sits a Big Bronc* is set in Texas shortly before the War Between the States, where a carpetbag governor organizes a group of hardcases to enforce his new laws. And in *Senorita Scorpion*, Chisos Owens is offered one thousand dollars to find the mysterious Scorpion, but his reasons have nothing to do with the reward.

**Dorchester Publishing Co., Inc.**
**P.O. Box 6640**                                     ___5303-9
**Wayne, PA 19087-8640**                        $4.99 US/$6.99 CAN

# A TRAIL TO WOUNDED KNEE

# TIM CHAMPLIN

In 1876 tensions run high on the prairie, where settlers push ever westward into Indian territories. Lt. Thaddeus Coyle is supposed to help keep the peace. Little does he know the greatest threat is from his commanding officer. Driven to disobey a direct order, Coyle winds up court-martialed and abandoned by his family. A ruined man, he finds his only friend is Tom Merritt—also known as Swift Hawk—a Lakota caught between his heritage and the white man's world. But when Coyle gets a job as U.S. Special Indian Agent and is sent to Wounded Knee, he and Swift Hawk will find themselves on opposite sides of the law on a prairie ready to go up in flames at the slightest spark.

---